Jack The Roper

AXEL HATCHETT MYSTERY VOL. 6

Steven LeRoy Nelson

BLOOD AND THUNDER PRESS

BLOOD AND THUNDER PRESS
3612 Sheffield Lane
Colorado Springs, CO 80907
www.bloodandthunderpress.com

ISBN-10: 1940469058
ISBN-13: 978-1-940469-05-8

To my little tongue and cheese sandwich.

1

I hate stakeouts. You can't drink, smoke, show a light, or even make any noise. It's kind of like being dead, I guess, except you still know what's going on around you. But stakeouts are a big part of being a gumshoe. Sometimes I wish I had a more interesting job, like being a hotdog vender.

This particular night I was earning a hundred bucks by sitting under a railroad bridge, eight o'clock on a nice mid-summer night. It was hard to believe that 1956 was more than half over already. I'd been hired to catch a kidnapper who would be showing up at ten to grab an envelope full of dough. Five-thousand smackers, to be exact. I'd wanted to get under the bridge early in case the punk who was picking up the money showed early to check the place out. Likely he'd show up right on time. All I had for company were a couple of dim streetlights, a trickling stream about a quarter of an inch deep, and the concrete pillar I was crouched behind.

The hours crawled by. I got cramps in all my muscles. The sky grew gradually darker and a cool breeze blew under the bridge and threatened to get chilly. I checked the gun in my pocket more than once to make sure I could get to it in a hurry. The moon was behind some clouds, and I had only the dim yellow streetlights to see by. The gurgle of the tiny stream was just loud enough to make it hard to hear anything else.

Around nine, a late passenger train passed over the bridge above me. If another one came along at ten, I wouldn't be able to hear a damned thing. Fortunately, that didn't happen. I kept looking at the luminous dial of my wristwatch. At almost exactly ten, I heard car tires crunching on the cinders that bordered the railroad tracks, but I couldn't see headlights or hear the car's engine. A minute later, I heard tentative footsteps and saw the beam of a flashlight.

I peeked around my pillar. Old Miss Agnes Weatherby, my client, dressed in some kind of slacks and a sweater, was headed right for the rock. She pushed it aside with one foot, found the note, and read it by the glow of her flashlight. The bunny-napper's ransom note had insisted that Miss Weatherby deliver the cash herself. She was paying out five-thousand clams for her kidnapped rabbit. You heard right, a bunny named Percy. I heard paper rustle, and figured Agnes was pushing the envelope full of money under the rock.

"Mr. Hatchett!" she whispered, a little too loudly. "Mr. Hatchett, are you here?"

Damn her, she was going to give me away.

"Quiet!" I whispered back. "I'm right here. Go back to your car and drive home."

"Yes, yes, of course."

She made her way back up the steep bank and in a while I heard her car tires crunching on the cinders again. I had my gun in my hand now, and I was all ears, just like a bunny. It seemed like a good twenty minutes later that I heard footsteps again, much heavier than Agnes's. The beam of a flashlight came on. I waited a moment then peered around my pillar again.

Someone wearing dark clothes and a ski mask was fussing with the rock. I crept up behind him. When I was only a couple of feet away, damned if some drunken yokel in a noisy jalopy didn't drive by on the road above. He let out some kind of cackle and the rabbit-napper in front of me straightened up and turned around. He saw me and I raised my gun. Too late; he was fast for a big guy. He swung his flashlight at my head and connected. It struck me just above my right ear, stunning me a little. Before I could recover, I got hit a second time, then a third.

I fell to my knees and tried to keep from passing out. I succeeded, but the guy who'd hit me was already clambering up the bank. I was dizzy, and when I tried to give chase, I fell down again and landed in the stream. I got up and followed him up the bank, reaching the top just in time to see one taillight of a dark vehicle disappear into the night. Like a sap, I'd parked my car near a warehouse a couple of blocks from the bridge; I hadn't wanted Percy's abductor to see it. I climbed bank down the bank and checked out the rock where Miss Weatherby had left the money. The envelope was gone.

By the time I got back to my car it was too late to give chase to Percy's kidnapper. I'd thoroughly messed things up. I hadn't caught whoever had taken the bunny; I'd let him get away with the five-thousand bucks, and I'd revealed that Agnes had hired a detective. That might make somebody mad. And Agnes might never see her rabbit again, which was my fault. On top of that, my head felt like a watermelon spiked with whiskey, and I had a fine collection of scrapes and bruises.

I drove until I found a payphone and gave Tracy, my wife, a quick call. I always try to keep Tracy apprised of my activities. Well, most of the time anyway. She answered on the first ring.

"Axe?"

"Yeah, it's me."

"Tell me you're all right. You didn't get shot again, did you?"

"No, just sapped with a big flashlight a few times, and I've got some bruises to show you."

"Oh, no! A rabbit did that to you?"

"Not a chance. I'm tougher than any rabbit. I'm even tougher than squirrels. The guy who came to pick up the ransom money roughed me up. I let him get away with Miss Weatherby's money, and I didn't even see what the guy looked like. He was wearing a ski mask. I just want you to know I'll be on this case a little longer, but we'll start our honeymoon on time. I promise."

"I believe you. Are you coming home?"

"I want to call the old lady and tell her what's up. She might want me to come over and talk to her. I'll bet she'll be mad."

"Don't worry. Old ladies aren't any tougher than squirrels."

"I hope that proves to be true. Listen, I've got to go. Don't wait up for me."

"I will if I want to. Me and the kittens. Get some ice for your head when you get a chance. I love you, you clumsy gumshoe."

"Love you, too, my little tongue and cheese sandwich."

I hung up and dialed Agnes's number.

"Weatherby residence."

It was Agnes herself. She must have just got home.

"Yeah, this is Axe Hatchett. I've got some bad news for you."

"You've found Percy? He's dead?"

She sounded frantic.

"No, no, no! I haven't seen hide nor hair of Percy. But whoever picked up the ransom money got away with it. He socked me with a flashlight. I didn't even get a decent look at him. I made a hash of everything. Listen, I'm not through with this case. I'll get the money back for you, and I'll find your rabbit-napper. It's going to take me some time, though. It might have to wait until I get back from my honeymoon."

She didn't say anything for several seconds, and when she did, her voice was the temperature of dry ice.

"Mr. Hatchett, do you mean to inform me that my money is gone and so is Percy's abductor? You've been very careless. It would seem I should have hired someone else. Someone competent."

"It was just rotten luck, that's all. I know what I'm doing. Trust me, everything will be fine."

"I doubt that. By the time your charming honeymoon is over, there will be no chance of getting to the bottom of things."

"I've still got a little time. Maybe tomorrow I can drop by your place and grill your relatives. I might be able to figure out who took Percy and the money."

"Why don't you come over now?"

"It's eleven o'clock at night."

"Everyone's still awake here. They're all night owls, I'm sorry to say."

"Don't a couple of them work?"

"Yes. Daisy and Margot, but they work the late shift at Sunny Sundown Rest Home."

"OK, I guess I can come over now."

"Do so, Mr. Hatchett. However, no one will want to talk to a detective. I'll introduce you as my cousin, Miles. Can you remember that name? I'll say you're one of Geneva's illegitimate children. She had several. Would that be all right?"

"I guess. Just call me Miles. Won't they catch on?"

"Probably not. They drink a good deal at night."

"Swell. I'm on my way."

While I drove over to Miss Weatherby's part of town, I thought about how this whole mess had gotten started. I'd been sitting in my office minding my own business for a change. I didn't have anybody else's business to mind. I looked out my dusty front window and saw a spanking new red convertible, a DeSoto, pull up to the curb. I smelled money. A tall old lady got out of the car and damned if she didn't walk right in my door.

"My dear Percy has been abducted," she told me. She had a prim way of talking, almost like a limey.

"Are you sure?" I asked. "Maybe Percy just got restless. Have you checked the nightclubs and the bowling alleys?"

"No. Percy is an angora rabbit, black and white."

"I guess that lets out the nightclubs. Have you checked your hedges?"

"Young man, you're impertinent."

"Sorry." Young man? I'm thirty-six, and I look and feel every year of it. Still. Miss Weatherby — that's the name she gave me — must have been eighty.

"I received a ransom note. The handwriting is atrocious, as is the grammar. I meant to bring the note with me, but I accidently left it at home. I am understandably flustered."

"Of course. My pet painted turtle once got lost under our calliope and I was a hopeless mess for a week."

She didn't like that. I got the impression there wasn't a whole lot she did like.

"Listen," I told her, "this doesn't sound like it's really in my line. Did you talk to the cops, or the dog catcher?"

"I do not want the police involved. I wasn't even going to hire a detective, but I talked with my brother-in-law, Primus Roan. I call him whenever I need good advice. He owns the dude ranch where you and your wife will be spending your honeymoon."

I was shocked. How the hell did this old lady know about me and Tracy's honeymoon plans? Miss Weatherby must have noticed the sappy look on my mug.

"Primus informed me that one of his clients— you—worked as a detective. Apparently, when you registered for reservations, you provided that information."

"Sure, the Carefree Buckaroo likes to know their guests have paying jobs."

"That's only prudent. Anyway, he suggested I look you up."

"Even though he knew I'd be heading up to his ranch to start my honeymoon? He must think I can wrap this case up in a hurry."

"You mean you think otherwise? I have reason to fear that one of my own relatives has taken Percy. Most of them don't work, and the ones who do are always wanting more money."

"I see. These blood-suckers live with you?"

"Yes. Billy, Ned, Margot, Daisy, and Hester. They all live in my house."

"Cozy. So what exactly do you want me to do?"

"Apprehend the kidnapper, and make certain I don't lose my five-thousand dollars. Of course, Percy's safety must come first."

Five thousand clams! For a bunny. I would have choked on my cigar if I'd been smoking one. The only reason I wasn't puffing on a stogie was because my wife's been giving me gentleman lessons. That's what happens when you get married — the leash gets tighter and shorter.

"You're telling me that whichever of your deadbeat relatives swiped Percy is asking for five-thousand bucks for his return? Rita Hayworth isn't worth that much. Well, maybe, if she's wearing red."

"That is the amount named in the ransom note. I stopped off at the bank on my way here. I have the money in my purse. I want to make certain Percy is not harmed. It would be just like Margot to chop off Percy's tail and mail it to me if I failed to cooperate."

"Margot sounds like a swell dame."

"Sometimes she forgets to take her medication. Margot and Daisy both work at the Sunny Sunset Retirement Home, but Margot has been talking about buying her own house, and Daisy wants a new car."

"Maybe they're in it together."

"Possibly. Then there is Hester. She's a clothes horse. She lives of off her boyfriends, who are legion. But Hester, poor girl, inherited the Weatherby nose, as well as the tendency towards rashes. Her gentlemen friends tend to be indigent."

I took a good gander at Miss Weatherby's honker. It was — to put it nicely, which a softhearted mug like me is apt to do — built along generous and showy lines. There was also a purple rash on her cheeks showing through the face powder.

"OK," I said, "what about these Ned and Billy characters? Possible suspects?"

"Oh, certainly. Ned has a war wound, he claims, and never works except for mowing my lawn. Billy gambles away the money I give him on horse and dog races."

"You mean races between a horse and a dog? I'd put my money on the horse."

"You are most facetious, Mr. Hatchett."

"Call me Axe. You'll have to forgive my attitude. I'm feeling kind of playful since I'm about to go on my belated honeymoon."

"Yes. Congratulations. I hope your new wife

isn't one of these silly things who'll run off with the first door-to-door salesman who has a Clark Gable mustache."

I bridled at that. "Tracy wouldn't do anything of the sort. She doesn't even like my mustache."

"Will you consider helping me or not? There are other private investigators in Quartz Quarry."

"They're bums. They couldn't find a fresh egg in a hen house. I'm your man, Miss Weatherby."

"How much will this cost me? I so hate talking about money."

"Sure, I know what you mean. I never talk about money except when I don't have any, which is most of the time. Let me make sure I understand what you want, Miss Weatherby. Your idea is to pretend to go along with the bunny-napper's demands and deliver the ransom. But then you're hoping I can figure a way to catch the guy — or the gal — when they come to pick up the money. You want Percy back in one piece, of course. And you want your five-thousand smackers back in your bank account. On top of that, you want me to collar the deadbeat relative who swiped Percy in the first place. Is all that correct?"

"Yes. Will you be able to do all that?"

"I'm your man. I generally charge thirty-five bucks an hour plus expenses. How about an even hundred? Nobody else will do it for less. I'll even throw in a free cigar."

"I do not smoke. One hundred dollars seems reasonable, if you do all the things I ask. I don't want the police involved, and I don't want any of my family members harmed. Agreed?"

"I might have to sock somebody in the jaw, but I'll be gentle. I'll use my padded brass knuckles."

"I won't hear of it. No rough stuff, as you detectives like to say."

"We've got ourselves a deal."

2

I thought the case would be no harder than a sunny stroll along a flower-bordered country lane. I forgot that sometimes bulls get loose on country lanes.

Miss Weatherby had given me her address and I found the house. One dim streetlight lit it up, and there was an even dimmer porch light. I parked the car—Tracy's plain-as-a-mud-fence Chevy—and walked along the broken brick path that led to the old two-storied Victorian house. I rang the bell and in less than a day the door was opened by a pudgy guy eating a pickle.

"You must be cousin Miles," he said, in a voice that a bullfrog would admire.

"Miles it is," I said.

I shook the hand that wasn't holding the pickle and stepped into an entry hall with an overburdened coat rack, a pie-crust table with a doily, and an old distorted mirror that made me look like I was swallowing my own ear.

"Name's Billy. Say, what happened to your face? You get in a bar fight? Happens to me all the time."

"Naw. I've been staying at the YMCA. I decided to give some guy a few boxing lessons. Turns out he didn't need them."

"Your mom, Geneva, is my Aunt Cora's stepsister," the guy told me. "The others are in the dining room. We was just having us some dessert, and some hooch. You like lumpy chocolate cake, or cheap gin?"

"I'll take a rain check. I'm trying to watch my chorus girl figure."

Billy showed me into a crowded room with a long table covered in a stained, yellowish cloth, too many chairs, a big glassed-in buffet thing, and a cobwebby chandelier with three of its bulbs burned out. My new kinfolk were seated at the table, with Agnes at the head. There was a collapsed-looking cake with brown frosting, and a cut-glass decanter that was half-filled with what was likely the promised gin.

"Cousin Miles," said Miss Weatherby, her dentures bared in a smile as big as a hippo's, "it's so good to see you. My, how you've grown!"

"Yeah. I was quite the little shaver the last time we met. I'm sure you're glad to see I finally grew into my ears."

"Your teeth look excellent," said a gangly dame of around thirty-five. She had stringy dark hair and was wearing a red cocktail dress and lots of cheap jewelry. Her dress said pricey hooker, but her eyes said you could buy her for a beer. "I have fine teeth myself. I don't even have to brush them. My mouth is naturally clean, like a dog's."

"This is Hester," said Agnes. "She's one of Rose and Roswell's children. You remember them?"

"Vaguely. It's been awhile."

"And this is Margot," she told me, gesturing at a swell-looking number with raven hair and glimmering eyes. She was wearing a too-tight blue sweater and too-tight black pants. There was something a little crazy in the smile she offered me.

"Welcome home, Miles," she said.

"Glad to be back with family," I said.

"I'm Ned," said a big guy around forty with frizzy hair. He was wearing overalls. "I'd stand up and shake hands with you, but I've got a bum leg. The war, you know."

The guy had a mouthful of chewing tobacco and he spit some of it into a coffee can on the table. The sound reminded me of something, but I couldn't think of what.

"And I'm Daisy, Miles," said a forty-ish damsel with broken veins around her nostrils and blood-shot eyes. She was swaying a little in her chair and she held a big glass of what was probably gin in one hand. "So, you're one of Geneva's kids. Did you ever find out who your dad was?"

"No. Rumor has it he was a traveling swimming pool salesman, but I never met the guy.

That's OK, I don't mind being a little bastard. Folks don't expect too much from you."

There were no more people to meet. None of them asked me about my busted face. Too polite, I guess. Daisy waved me to a chair and offered me some cake and my choice of whiskey or gin. Billy offered me a pickle, and Ned held out his pouch of Redman and asked if I cared for a chew.

"Thanks, but I had a big supper," I told them. "I'll stick with my cigars, if no one minds."

"I mind," said Margot. "Only brutal men smoke cigars. Are you a brutal man, Miles?"

"Not so you'd notice. Say, I wouldn't mind a nip of that gin." I thought it might help my headache.

"Sure," said Hester. "Let's have one together."

She found a big tumbler and poured three or four fingers of gin into it. I drank it down like a hero and actually started feeling better. I looked around at the noisy band of hooligans and wondered how the proper Miss Weatherby put up with them. They all seemed pretty sloshed. Ned started telling me a war story, but Margot interrupted him.

"Ned wants to tell you about his war wound," she said, rolling her crazy eyes. "He fell out of a Jeep while delivering some general's laundry."

"That's not how it was," broke in Ned, turning even redder than he'd already been. "You're just jealous because you don't have a war wound."

"I could have been in the service," hissed Margot.

"Sure, but they wouldn't let you dames fight. Good thing, too, or we would have lost the war."

Margot lunged across the table at Ned, a fork in her hand, but the war hero jumped out of his chair and backed against the wall. He seemed pretty spry for a guy with a bum leg.

"Children!" shouted Agnes. "I'll have none of this fighting. It's time you all went to your rooms."

"It's too early, Auntie," complained Hester. "I want to get to know Miles better."

She fluttered her fake eyelashes at me. I tried not to notice.

"Does anyone want more cake?" asked Daisy, pouring more gin into her glass.

Nobody answered. Margot had calmed down, and Ned returned to his chair.

"You staying with us?" Billy asked me.

"Of course he is," said Agnes. "He's family."

I wondered if she'd forgotten I wasn't really a relative of hers.

"Is your luggage in your car?" asked Hester, a leer on her lipsticked mouth. "I'll help you carry it to your room."

Ned noisily spat tobacco juice into his coffee can. That's when I remembered where I'd heard that same sound before. I got up from the table.

"Thanks for reminding me, cousin Hester," I said. "Damned if I didn't leave my suitcase at the Y. I better go get it right now before some bum swipes it."

I promised everyone I'd be back and headed for the front door. As I'd hoped, Agnes followed me out onto the porch.

"Mr. Hatchett!" Agnes whispered, fiercely. "Where are you going? What are you doing?"

"My job's done, Miss Weatherby. Ned's your man. He stole your bunny and your money."

"How could you possibly know that?"

"When he was under the bridge, swiping the ransom money, I heard him spit tobacco juice. It was exactly the same kind of sloshy spit I've heard him make twice in this house. Whoever hit me with his flashlight had some size to him, like Ned. Does he have a car?"

"Only an old pickup truck. He and Billy own it together. They keep it held together with baling wire. Why?"

"Where's the truck now?"

"Parked on the street. It's right there, between my DeSoto and that other car."

The other car was Tracy's Chevy.

"Can they see us from the house?" I asked.

"Not if they're still in the dining room."

I grabbed my flashlight from the Chevy's glove box and took a good look at Ned and Billy's truck. It was an old Ford Model A, a rust bucket. Those old Model A's only came with one taillight. I studied the tires with my light. They were pretty well worn, but I found some gravel stuck in the treads.

"That clinches it," I said, to Agnes. "The car that

the rabbit-napper was driving only had one tail-light, and the gravel in the tire treads matches what was next to the railroad tracks. If I were you, Miss Weatherby, I'd have Ned's bedroom searched. I think you'll find an envelope full of money. Listen, it's eleven-thirty. I've got to get some shuteye."

"You can't leave now. What about Percy?"

"I'm sure Percy's just fine. Get Ned to tell you where the rabbit's hidden. Sic Margot on Ned."

"I'll call you if anything comes up, Mr. Hatchett. If something's happened to Percy for instance. Thank you for your help."

"It was a pleasure."

I got in my car and took off. I wanted to put some distance between me and my new cousins. And I wanted to rest my sore head, and have Tracy kiss it.

3

I had some whiskey when I got home, and Tracy made a pot of coffee. She cleaned up an ugly cut on my temple, and even the two kittens sat at my feet and mewed. I felt pretty pampered.

"I'd say you earned your hundred dollars, you poor thing," said Tracy.

I'd told Tracy all about my bunny-napping case as soon as Miss Weatherby had hired me. I was happy about it. Tracy wasn't.

"You're taking on a new case? This close to our honeymoon?" she'd complained. "What's wrong with you, Axe? You'll ruin everything."

"The job's a cinch," I'd said. "It won't take me more than a couple of hours."

"You always say that, and you're always wrong."

We'd been talking in Ben and Allie's Sandwich Shop. It's in the same building as my office, and we rent the apartment upstairs. Tracy works in the sandwich shop. It all works out pretty slick.

"I won't mess up our honeymoon, precious," I told her. "I promise."

It was a slow time of the day for people buying sandwiches. Tracy was mopping the white linoleum floor. She accidently mopped over my shoes. What the hell, they needed polishing anyway.

"You and your pretty dames!" said Tracy. "You can't ever say no to them."

"Agnes Weatherby is pushing eighty. She's not exactly a heart-breaker."

"We'll be late for our own honeymoon. I'll go without you. It'll be like being stood up at my own wedding."

She started bawling. But she wasn't through talking, not by a long shot. Tracy isn't one of those girls who are cute when they're mad. Her face turns red, her eyes squinch up, and her mouth opens as wide as an alligator's

"Everything will be fine, fruit cup," I told her.

"No it won't. You're going to let a rabbit spoil our plans. We've been saving up over six month for our honeymoon. I've been waiting all this time for us to go to a dude ranch. Now you're letting some old lady's bunny screw things up. Why did that Primus Roan cowboy recommend you anyway? He knew you had plans."

"Settle down. I took the case because I thought we could use the extra money for souvenirs and sugar lumps for the horses. Besides, we'll need some extra cash in case I get bit by a cow and end up in the hospital."

"That'd be just like you to get bit by a cow, you big goof. And look at your hat! How many guys do you know with bullet holes in their hats? You're lucky it's not been your head."

"Yeah. You're right."

I could tell she was winding down. She was out of breath, and a smile was tickling at her lips.

"OK," she said. "Go ahead and rescue the rabbit for the poor old lady. But don't waste any time. And don't let some smart aleck use you for target practice."

"I don't think the bunny's packing heat."

She'd stopped being mad, and later I went out to sit under a railroad bridge and wait for some dope to pick up Percy's ransom money. Now I was home again, with a bandaged head, a hundred bucks, and two young cats fussing at a hole in one of my socks.

"I never want to see another member of the Weatherby family as long as I live," I told Tracy. "That family's poison ivy and loco weed combined."

It was after midnight before we got to bed. My wife had to be up and in the sandwich shop at six. She worked long hours, and I looked forward to the time when I was making better money and Tracy could take some time off. She'd been working in restaurants since she was a kid.

I'd been chasing dollars as a shamus for several years and had damned little to show for it. Not for the first time, I thought about getting into another line of work. Still, there's something about being a private eye that gets in your blood, kind of like lead poisoning.

At five o'clock in the morning, the damned phone started ringing. While I struggled to wake up, Tracy jumped out of bed and answered it. A moment later, she was back in the bedroom.

"It's for you," she said. "I told her you were sleeping off a bruising, but she insists on talking to you. She sounds old."

Damn! Miss Weatherby. I staggered into the living room and grabbed the phone.

"Yeah?" I said.

"Mr. Hatchett? This is Agnes Weatherby. I have news about Percy. You were right about Ned. He caught Billy searching his bedroom and made quite a fuss. Billy and Margot managed to tie him to a chair. Ned refused to admit he'd taken the money, though it was found in his dresser drawer, under his pistol. He wouldn't tell us where Percy was until Hester threatened to scorch his bare feet with a blowtorch. Do you have family, Mr. Hatchett?"

"Yeah, but they live in other states."

"You're fortunate. Apparently, Ned had a confederate, some gambling and drinking companion who helped him. The miscreant has a sister in Meandering Spruce. He drove Percy down there earlier in the week."

"That's a hundred miles from here."

"Yes. Ned wanted to make sure Percy couldn't

be found without help."

"Well, I guess you'll have to drive down to Meandering Spruce and collect your rabbit."

"I can't go down there by myself. I'm afraid of Ned's confederate. His name is Pug. I can't face a person with a name like that. I want a man with me."

"Take Billy."

"That had been my intention, but Billy has a job interview later this morning."

"I thought the guy didn't like to work."

"He's turned over a new leaf."

"Sure he has. Listen, wait until his interview is over and then drive down with him to fetch Percy."

"I can't wait that long. I must have my Percy back. What if they've starved him?"

"I'm sure he's fine. Listen, what do you want from me?"

"I'm sure you've guessed. I want you to accompany me to Meandering Spruce."

"I can't do it. Sorry."

"I'll pay you a hundred dollars."

"Just a second."

I thought about it. Tracy was hanging around the phone, pretending she wasn't listening. I covered the mouthpiece.

"Tracy, Miss Weatherby will give me another hundred dollars if I drive her over to Meandering Spruce to pick up her bunny. It's easy money, and we could use it on our honeymoon. What do you say?"

Tracy shook her head.

"You'll get sapped again. I want my husband in one piece when we go on our honeymoon."

"But it's almost daylight already. I'll just be taking a country drive with a little old lady. I'll be careful. You think I'm going to let myself get waylaid two days in a row?"

"How long will the trip take you?"

"A few hours. I should be back before noon."

"I wish I could go with you. All right, Axe, but don't let any of your crazy new cousins go along with you."

"It'll just be me and Miss Weatherby."

I spoke into the phone again.

"Miss Weatherby? You've got yourself a deal."

"Oh, I'm so relieved. Hurry over. I'll be waiting on the porch."

"I'll be at your place as soon as I can."

I hung up.

Tracy made coffee while I climbed into my clothes. I was out the door in less than twenty minutes.

When I parked my car behind Agnes's DeSoto, I saw her standing on her porch. She came down the steps as I got out of the Chevy.

"We'll take my car," she told me. "It's newer. I don't want any motoring mishaps."

She gave me the keys and I helped her into the car, then got in behind the wheel. When I tried starting the DeSoto, nothing happened. Nothing.

"You been having trouble with this buggy?" I asked.

"Absolutely not. Billy keeps it in good running order."

I got out and popped the hood. The damned battery had been stolen. I gave Agnes the news.

"One of the hooligan neighbor children must have taken it. Some of them are quite ill mannered. What shall we do now?"

"We'll take my jalopy. It runs fine."

We switched cars and were soon on our way.

The drive from Quartz Quarry to Meandering Spruce is a pretty one. The road winds along through the mountains, with the river on one side and forest on the other. It would have been a pleasant trip except for two things: my empty belly, and Agnes's constantly-spoken fears for Percy's health.

"The little guy will be OK," I told her, for the twentieth time. "Ned knows how much you care for that rabbit."

"But does he care himself? He stole five-thousand dollars from me, and he's made these last few days very harrowing. I have half a mind to throw him out."

"You mean you haven't? You didn't show him the door and tell him how to use it?"

"Not yet. I've told you before, I'm a woman who can't say no."

"Start practicing."

When we finally pulled into Meandering

Spruce—a sleepy little town that made its money off of orchards and the occasional tourist—it was close to nine. I'd forgotten how long it takes to drive through the mountains. A hundred miles is a long ways. Agnes fished an address out of her purse and we asked for directions from a cop who was standing around on a street corner waiting for a crime to happen. The house we were looking for was a shabby-looking duplex on the far edge of town. We got out of the car and headed for the front door together. Agnes was practically gasping with anticipation.

I rang the bell and the door was opened almost at once by a middle-aged fat woman with unfortunate hair.

"We're here for the rabbit," I told her.

"About damn time. I'll go get him," she said, and closed the door.

I turned to Miss Weatherby.

"Do you want to press charges?" I asked.

"Certainly not! I only want this nightmare over with. I'm not pressing charges against anyone, not even Ned. He's family."

"Pug and his girlfriend aren't your family."

"I dare not involve them with the law. Ned might get caught-up in the investigation."

"Suit yourself."

The door opened again, and the woman with the coonskin hair pushed a big cardboard box out onto the cement stoop. Agnes leaned over and undid the box flaps. A pink-nosed rabbit blinked out at her and wiggled its nose.

"Percy! Darling! Are you all right?"

She pulled the bunny out of his box and hugged him to her lavender-scented bosom.

"I had nothing to do with any of this," said the fat dame. "It was all Pug's idea. Him and that Ned. I swear."

"It doesn't matter, dear," Agnes told her. "You aren't in any trouble. Thank you for watching after my Percy."

"I gave him some canned spinach, but he wouldn't eat it."

"I should think not. I've got a proper meal for him in my purse."

We got back into the Chevy and I drove around looking for an eatery. Agnes held Percy on her lap and fed him from a sack of greens she had stuffed in her purse. Finally, we hove into view of Mitsy's Burger Palace, a little shack by the side of the road where you could sit in your car and eat a lot of grease. I demolished two cheeseburgers and a mountain of fries, plus two cups of coffee. Agnes said she was too nervous to eat.

"I can't thank you enough, Mr. Hatchett," she told me, while she kept stuffing lettuce and radish tops into Percy's willing mouth. "I must admit, I had my doubts about you for a while there."

"That's OK, so did I. Listen, let's head home."

I pulled the car back onto the main road and we began the long drive to Quartz Quarry. Despite the coffee, I was feeling pretty tired, and my skull was still giving me fits. Agnes fished in her purse and brought out two hundred dollar bills and pushed them at me.

I shook my head.

"The deal was for one hundred," I said.

"You earned the extra. I know you got hurt, and you were put to a great deal of bother. Please."

"Nope. A hundred's plenty. I appreciate the offer, but no thanks. By the way, is Percy housebroken?"

"Of course he is. He can even make barking noises like a dog. He's quite exceptional."

We got into Quartz Quarry about twelve-thirty, and I drove to Miss Weatherby's place. Her DeSoto was no longer parked at the curb.

"My goodness, what's become of it?" she asked. Her eyes narrowed and she got a prim look on her face. "It's that scoundrel, Billy, I'll bet. Job interview indeed! You know what he's done?"

"Let me guess. He removed your car battery while everyone was asleep, and then as soon as we drove out of sight, he put it back. He's off joyriding someplace."

"I think you are entirely correct. He's stolen my car! Oh, Mr. Hatchet, could you track him down for me? I'll have Ned give you a list of Billy's favorite bars and haunts."

I shook my head so hard I could feel the sponge I use for a brain sloshing around.

"No. I've done enough. Recovered your money,

identified the rabbit-napper, and helped you get back Percy. I'm done. I'm ready for a week in the high lonesome, with no detective work whatsoever. That's my final word."

"Of course, if you insist. Tell your blushing bride hello for me. Perhaps I can send Daisy out to look for Billy. She's fairly reliable, when she's sober."

4

By the time I got back home, close to one, I was beat. The cut on my head was throbbing and the burgers I'd had for lunch were fighting it out in my belly. All I wanted was a hot shower and a long, long, nap. I was glad we didn't have to drive up to the dude ranch until tomorrow morning. I parked the Chevy in front of my office and then ducked inside. I was carrying too much cash on me. My office had previously been inhabited by a lawyer, now retired. He'd left a wall safe—I guess he couldn't figure out how to take it with him— behind a big picture of George Washington. I guess the painting was supposed to put the shyster lawyer's clients at ease. He'd chop down cherry trees, but he wouldn't lie about it.

The blinds on my front window were pulled down. The place was dim. I shut the door and flipped on the light switch. The ceiling light came on and then went out with a popping noise. Damn! I started over to my desk where there was one of those lamps with a neck like a crane's. Before I'd taken more than two steps, there were a couple of flashes of bright light and the sound of two shots. I hit the floor.

Before I got my snub-nosed thirty-eight in my hand, the shooter was making for the side door of my office. He fired one more shot in my direction and slipped out the door, banging it behind him. I was up off the floor in a second, but by the time I got the side door open, the guy was gone. He'd headed down the little alleyway that runs along the side of the building. I considered chasing him, but—what the hell?—he'd just shoot me.

My front door opened and Tracy came in, shouting: "Axe! Are you all right? I heard shots!"

"I'm fine, princess," I said, dusting off my clothes. My office floor isn't as clean as it could be. Who has time for sweeping?

"What happened?" Tracy asked, almost jumping into my arms.

"Some mug with a gun broke into my office and threw a few slugs at me. I'm OK." I checked myself to make sure that was true. I didn't find any bullet holes or blood. I was damned lucky my light bulb had gone out when it did. I pointed at the ceiling light. "I'm keeping that bulb. It saved my life."

"We'll have it stuffed and put it on the mantel."

"We don't even have a fireplace."

"Well, let's have one put in. You sure you're OK?"

"Never better."

"Why was the guy shooting at you?" Tracy was trying to lead me to the front door.

"I'm not sure, but I have an idea. I think my new cousin Ned might be the shooter. He's kind of crazy."

"Let's call the cops."

"Let's not. They'll waste time and we don't want to be late for our honeymoon. I'll take care of this business when we get back home, believe me."

"No. We'll call the cops. What if the guy comes back for a second try? Did one of those bullets hit your head?"

"We'll leave it for later," I said.

I started looking around for bullet holes. Two of the slugs had buried themselves in the doorframe. The third one had punched a hole in the ceiling.

"Some marksman," I said.

"Don't complain."

I went over and checked the side door. It looked like my would-be assassin had jimmied it open with a crowbar. There was no time to call a locksmith. I pushed a big bookcase over in front of it.

"Come on, Tracy, let's leave this dump."

Outside, we met Ben and Allie coming from the sandwich shop. Their eyes looked as big as saucers. They're a round little couple from Romania or some damned place. They're nice folks.

"What happened?" asked Ben.

"Nothing," I said. "Some idiot got his dates mixed up. He thought it was the fourth of July. No harm done."

"Did someone shoot at your head?" asked Allie. She pointed at the hat I was holding in my hand. I looked at it. Damned if there wasn't another couple of holes through it. That made four. A few months earlier, somebody had shot at me and Tracy while we stood in front of this same building. I was beginning to think we lived in the wrong neighborhood.

"We will call the police," said Ben.

"Not now," I said. "I'll handle this when me and Tracy get back from our honeymoon. There's no need to bother the boys in blue yet. This can wait."

"Of this you are sure?" asked Allie.

"Everything's fine," I said.

"You could have been killed," said Tracy. "I wish you'd find a safer line of work."

"But there's nothing as exciting! I like my job. Let's step into the sandwich shop. I could use a cup of coffee."

We all piled into the place and Ben brought me a big cup of coffee.

"Would you like a sandwich?" Ben asked me.

"No thanks. I ate on the road. I had a couple of lively hamburgers. Too bad the gunman didn't shoot me in the belly, maybe that would have made the burgers stop fighting each other."

"Don't even say that, mister," said Tracy.

"You're lucky you didn't catch your death of lead poisoning."

"The guy was a lousy shot."

"He shot your hat. Good thing the slug bounced off your thick skull," said Tracy. "How'd you make out with the bunny?"

"Swell. I got the furry little guy back in one piece. I recovered the ransom money, and pegged the guy who swiped the rabbit. And we've got two-hundred smackers to show for it. All's well that ends well."

"You look pretty worn-out, spud gut. Better take a nap." Tracy smiled big. "I've got great news."

"You invented a new sandwich?"

"Better than that, buster. I called the Carefree Buckaroo to make sure everything was all set for our stay."

"You called the dude ranch? That's a long distance call. We ain't made of money, cherry lips."

"You just made two-hundred dollars!"

"Yeah, you've got a point. What's the news?"

"The folks who were staying in the cabin we're going to have left early. We can go up today. They won't charge us extra."

"Why'd they leave early?" I'm always suspicious. "Did the horses bite them, or was it the food that drove them away?"

"I didn't ask. What difference does it make? Hurry and take your nap. Ben and Allie are letting me off early. One of their daughters is coming in to work the rest of my shift. I'll pack while you sleep. OK?"

I didn't think a short nap was going to do much for me. It would take several hours to drive up to the dude ranch. We'd be taking our truck, a 1937 Studebaker. It'd been Ben and Allies. They'd bought a new panel truck and had the name of their sandwich shop painted on the sides. They offered to sell the older truck to me and Tracy for a song, so I sang them one. I get detective work up in the mountains sometimes, and I knew a truck would come in handy. Tracy hated driving it, so that would leave me to drive to the Carefree Buckaroo.

I wanted to tell Tracy that I wouldn't be up to traveling until the morning, but I can't say no to the kid.

"Swell," I said. "That's great news."

I climbed the stairs to our apartment. There seemed to be a whole lot of them. The kittens ran to greet me and I put my shower off long enough to play with them. I still call them kittens, but they're mostly grown. Great big toms with a natural viciousness you usually have to pay extra for. I got out of my dirty clothes and limped to the shower while the cats tore the place apart. By the time Tracy came up, I was in bed asleep. I woke up just long enough to hear her come in. It seemed like only five minutes later that my wife shook me awake.

"What?" I said, sleepily. "Is the place on fire?"

"No. We'll save the fire for our honeymoon nights. Speaking of which, we'd better get going. I know you don't like driving in the mountains after dark. I've got the packing done. You've been asleep for hours."

"You kidding me?"

"No. You've been snoring like a drunken sailor."

"Jeez, maybe that's why I feel seasick. Let me get up and make some coffee."

"I already did. I'll bring you a cup, just the way you like it, with a dead fly in it."

"Just like at Rocko's. You ever miss the place?"

"Don't be a sap. My only good memory of working there was the day you walked in."

"The day I walked in you were mean to me."

"I was just playing hard to get, like the sappy dames in the movies. You weren't exactly a sweetheart yourself."

"I was just being shy. Actually, I thought you were about as appetizing as Rocko's greasy chili."

"So why'd you keep coming back?"

"I was hoping the chow would toughen up my gut."

"You're lying. You couldn't get enough of me."

"And I never will, my little slushy snow cone."

I drank my coffee—two cups—and then loaded up the truck with our suitcases, the litter box, and some sandwiches to eat on the road. We carried down Eben and Mayhew and put them in the truck cab with us. They climbed onto the back of the seat and looked out the window and started making zoo noises.

"They're excited," said Tracy. "Wait until they see their first horses."

"You seem pretty excited yourself."

"Of course I am! And so are you, you big faker."

Tracy was right when she'd said I hate driving in the mountains at night, but we still had plenty of daylight when we started out. The roads were decent until we reached the small town of Quail Eye, then the blacktop turned to dirt, and the roads got narrow, crooked, and rutted. I was glad we'd taken the truck. The whole time I was driving, I'd been checking the rearview mirror for Ned's Model A truck. He must have driven it when he visited me at my office. It'd be just like the idiot to follow me for a second try at ventilating my hide. However, I didn't see any sign of an old pickup truck behind us.

"Why do you keep looking in the mirror?" Tracy asked. "Just admiring your broken nose?"

"I'm making sure the guy who shot at me isn't following us. I don't trust him."

"No? You're an awfully suspicious guy. I'll keep an eye out too. What kind of a jalopy are we looking for?"

"A dark Model A pickup. It's hard to say what color it is. It might have started out as blue or brown, but the years haven't been good to it."

It was full dark and the sky was showing a million stars by the time our headlights lit up the Carefree Buckaroo sign. It featured a goofy-looking cowpoke with a toothy smile. Some gun-happy galoot had shot a few holes through the sign, peppering the cowboy's nose and ruining his smile something awful.

"That's mean," said Tracy.

"I guess cowboys will be cowboys."

I turned into the driveway, clattered across a cattle guard and through an open gate, and followed the rutted road up to the ranch. It looked like a cramped ghost town squatting in the starlight. All of the structures were made of logs with the bark still on. They included a barn, a long low structure that was probably the chow house, a quaint two-storied house, and half a dozen pint-sized cabins. The roofs were sway-backed, and some of the latticed windows had been patched up with oiled paper. A big light on a pole lit up the buildings and the graveled parking area. I parked next to a DeSoto that looked awfully damned familiar. It couldn't be. What the hell would Billy—or Miss Weatherby—be doing up here? I grunted something under my breath.

"What'd you say?" asked Tracy.

"Nothing. Happy honeymoon."

There were lights in some of the cabin windows, and one in the chow house. The present batch of dudes were scheduled to leave early in the morning. The new dudes would show up a little later.

"Our cabin is number six," said Tracy.

"End of the row, huh? Listen, I'll carry our suitcases over to the cabin if you want to go to the long building with the light on in it and fetch the key. Then we'll unload our winsome boys. I don't want them getting loose. They might kill an elk or something."

"I love elk, especially with gravy. Tell the cats to kill two. I'll go get the key."

I got our suitcases out of the back of the truck — they were covered with road dust — and lugged them down to number six. A little yellow porch light was on. The porch was about the size of a doormat. I lit up a cigar and headed for the chow house. Tracy met me about halfway there. She had a big smile on her face.

"Our very own cozy mountain cabin," she said, handing me an old key with a wooden tag attached. "It's so romantic."

"Wait until we get inside," I warned. "The place could be full of barn owls and snakes."

"Naw. Maybe a packrat or two."

I stuck the key into a rusty lock and opened the door. It creaked. I felt around for a light switch and found one on the wall. A bare bulb lit up a tiny room that looked cozy in a derelict kind of way. There was a double bed with a crazy quilt spread on it, a tarnished brass horsehead lamp on a rickety nightstand, a hook rug on the pine floor, and a scarred cedar chest under the one window. There was a closet smelling of cedar, with some bent coat hangers in it. There was a big pickle jar with faded wild flowers on the cedar chest.

"Home sweet home," I said.

Tracy threw herself into my arms and kissed me no more than a dozen times. Well, maybe a baker's dozen.

"Our very own honeymoon cottage!" she said. "And we can sleep in tomorrow because the new guests might check in late. Breakfast is at ten o'clock."

"Who'd you talk to in the big house?"

"A buckaroo named Panhandle. Kind of pasty-faced for a cowboy, but he had the right kind of hat."

"Big guy? Soft around the middle? Stupid looking?"

"How'd you know?" She gave me one of her suspicious squints.

"I think I met him when he was still calling himself Billy. He's one of the loons that was living with Miss Weatherby. He might have stolen her car. I saw it in the parking lot. His uncle is Miss Weatherby's brother-in-law. I guess that means Billy is somehow related to Primus Roan."

"Axe, don't go sticking your bloodhound nose into any more trouble."

"I won't. I'm just wondering why Billy — Panhandle — is up here. He's not much for working, I hear."

"He told me he just got here today."

"Swell. Let's rescue the cats."

41

We went back out to the truck. I grabbed the litter box while Tracy corralled the cats and carried them, mewing, to our cabin. Tracy put them down on the floor and I put out their food, then looked around for a source of water for them.

"Doesn't this place have a bathroom?" I asked.

"No. We're roughing it, remember? Panhandle said there are outhouses in back of the cabins, and a pump, and a shack to shower in."

"And for this we passed up Niagara Falls. Great. I guess I'll go pump some water for Eben and Mayhew. I hope the well's not poisoned."

Outside, the stars were still making a show, and it was getting pretty chilly. I pumped water into the cat dish and went back to the cabin. Tracy had already changed into a pink nightgown I'd never seen before. It did nice things to her curves.

"Welcome back, cowboy," she said. "The bed looks kind of lumpy, but I don't think we'll mind. We can massage it into shape."

"Sounds like fun."

I grabbed her and kissed her. The rest of the night went by pretty fast.

The next morning, our tinny wind-up alarm clock went off at nine. I slapped it quiet and we stayed in bed a little longer. Then Eben and Mayhew got in the bed and wouldn't leave us alone.

"I think they like it in the mountains," said Tracy.

"Who doesn't like the mountains?"

We got dressed, visited the smelly privies out

back, and moseyed over to the grub house. There were a bunch of cars in the parking lot. I looked at the license plates. Texas, Kansas, New Jersey, Illinois, and a couple of fellow Coloradans. Some of the cars no doubt belonged to the dudes who were leaving.

"It's a beautiful day," said Tracy.

I couldn't argue with that. The sun was well up in the sky, the birds were making noise, and the air smelled like it was brand new.

Four more greenhorns — two couples — joined us as we walked in the door of the chuck house. Inside there was a third couple, already cued up at a food-burdened buffet table, with tin plates in their hands. We all joined them.

The room was big and featured knotty pine paneling and varnished logs for pillars and beams. We loaded our plates with scrambled eggs, bacon, toast, coaster-sized pancakes, and homemade doughnuts. We took our full plates over to a couple of long pine tables — like outsized picnic tables — and went to work on the grub. The whole gang — including me, I'm sorry to say — was dressed in spanking new Western apparel. Jeans, shiny new cowboy boots, fancy checked shirts with flap pockets and pearl buttons. Two of the men wore pristine cowboy hats. I wore my old fedora with the bullet holes through it.

There was a clattering of knives and forks and tin cups and hasty, hearty, introductions. Before we got down to calling each other partner, a pair of swinging doors at one end of the room opened and a pretty cowgirl and a hulking cowman appeared with big trays of more food. The girl was sunny-haired and freckled, a smile as big as all outdoors on her face. The hulking guy, white as a fish belly, was Billy.

"Welcome folks," said the shapely cow miss. "Eat up all you can. We've got a busy day planned for you. I'm Sissy Dell, and this fellow is Panhandle. We'll be taking care of the cooking for you. In a minute here, Mr. Breedlaw, that's my uncle, is going to come talk to you about the Carefree Buckaroo."

"Howdy folks!" bellowed Billy—Panhandle. He saw me and grew even more pale. He ducked his head and quickly made his way back to the kitchen.

Sissy Dell topped off our coffee cups, and chattered away like a ground squirrel.

"Do we get to pick out our own horses?" Tracy asked her.

"Well, ma'am, that's the wrangler's job. You'll have to talk to him. His name's Hawk Luster, and he's handsome enough to turn the head of any heifer." She gently shook a finger at us. "Mind you watch your ladies, gents."

With a laugh as tinkly as a bicycle bell, she left us to our chow and went back through the swinging doors. Her hips were swinging too.

I had no time to think about Panhandle. I heard the sound of tires on gravel and looked out the latticed window. A tan Ford, with a sheriff's star in white on the door, rolled into the parking lot. I figured they were here to collect Panhandle, but I figured wrong. A big guy with a cowboy hat, a tan uniform, and a tin star, got out of the driver's side of the Ford. A smaller guy, with a bigger hat, maybe a deputy, got out of the passenger's side. And then a lanky guy with silver hair, a turquoise shirt, and a bolo tie, came out of nowhere and greeted the lawmen. The three of them talked for a minute, silver hair pointed his finger, and they all went off in that direction.

"What's all that about," said a round, sandy-haired, guy who'd introduced himself as Curt Halsey, hardware, Flummers, Iowa. His wife, pudgy and curly haired, was named Mabel. "Think it's cattle rustlers?"

"Maybe it's a show put on for us dudes," guessed a woman—not bad looking in a lanky, ponytailed, kind of way—whose name was Betsy. She was married to Walter, a long drink of ice water with no flesh on him to speak of.

"No, something's up," said Dr. Rumdab, a guy too old to be riding horses or to be married to the pixy-faced Lilly he'd introduced as his wife.

"Maybe some steer was caught jaywalking," I said. The comment got more of a laugh than it deserved.

Sissy Dell and Panhandle rushed back into the room. The girl's smile was still in place but her eyes looked frantic. Panhandle was carrying a guitar. From his expression and actions, I figured he wasn't on the sheriff's list— yet.

"There's way more food, folks," said Sissy Dell. "Eat up! Mr. Breedlaw's going to be a little late. I'm sorry. While we're waiting for him, me and Panhandle are going to sing you a few cowboy songs."

Panhandle started strumming the guitar, and damned if he couldn't actually play. Sissy Dell sang "What's Become of the Punchers" in a sweet voice, but she had to work hard on the low notes. They finished the song and started in on the "Tennessee Stud", but Dr. Rumdab interrupted them.

"Why is the sheriff here?" he demanded, in a loud voice.

"Sheriff Fish is here to talk to Mr. Breedlaw," said Sissy Dell. "There's been a little accident."

"What kind of accident," asked Rumdab.

"None of your damned business," said Panhandle. "Eat your pancakes."

"See here!" said Rumdab.

Sissy Dell elbowed Panhandle. "Panhandle's just upset because of the misfortune. Mr. Breedlaw will explain things when he gets done talking to the sheriff."

"Is everything OK, Miss?" asked Curt, the Iowa hardware man. He looked scared.

"Everything's just fine, folks," said Sissy Dell, brightly, but her heart wasn't in it.

"A guy's dead, that's all," growled Panhandle.

"Mercy!" said curly-haired Mabel, adding a little squeak. "How'd he die? Did a horse throw him?"

"Just go on with your breakfast, folks," said Sissy Dell. "What do you think of our doughnuts?"

"The guy died with a rope around his neck," said Panhandle. Sissy Dell elbowed him again, this time hard enough to make him grunt.

The front door opened and a tall cowboy walked in, holding his big hat in his hand. He was something to look at. Floppy raven hair, lonesome steely eyes, a cleft chin and a hawk nose, and lots of suntan. He was dressed all in black, with silver buttons on his shirt, and a white kerchief around his bull neck, held in place by a little silver steer's head. He wore a black, tooled, gun belt, with a pearl handled, nickel-plated, Colt revolver peeking out of the holster. His boots were shiny black with silver toes. Pure Hollywood.

"Folks, my name's Hawk Luster," he said, in a low voice just made for soothing jumpy night herds. The ladies in the room all sighed, even Tracy. "We got ourselves a situation. Ranch life can be kind of harsh. One of our wranglers met his maker last night. Mr. Breedlaw run across him a little over an hour ago. Poor Brice has gone to his reward. I reckon he was trying to rope old Whitey, a wild stallion that comes in the night and runs off our mares. I can't tell you more than that. It's the sheriff's business now. I reckon as soon as you've finished your mighty fine breakfast, you folks should be going back to your cabins. Them's the sheriff's orders. Nobody's allowed to leave the ranch."

"This is outrageous!" said Rumdab. "Before I made our reservations I was assured that the West was no longer wild."

"We still got some rough edges," said Hawk.

"Rough edges, indeed. I'll be calling my lawyer."

"The death was an accident, wasn't it?" asked Curt, pulling his wife closer to him.

"I reckon the sheriff will decide that," said Hawk.

We all started getting to our feet, and there was a lot of chatter. Tracy gave me a look that said, "Stay out of this."

"Let's go back to our cabins, everyone," I said, raising my voice. "Everything's going to be just fine. No doubt they're just looking into the death to make sure it was an accident. Maybe the sheriff will want to talk to us, but it won't amount to much. Let's just take it easy. We'll be riding horses and singing songs before you know it."

For some reason, the idiots seemed to believe me. They quieted down and started filing out the door. Hawk Luster gave me a nod of thanks.

"Just wait in your cabins until we come get you," Hawk told us.

We muttered and crept our way to our broken-down cabins. When Tracy and me were inside, with the door safely closed, she turned on me.

"You stay out of this, Mr. Big Shot detective. If

somebody's been murdered it's none of your business."

"I couldn't agree with you more. It's just my bad luck that some poor cowpoke got knocked off on our honeymoon. I'm keeping my nose out of it, cowgirl. Don't think otherwise."

5

Tracy grabbed me and hugged and kissed me. She kept it up until there was a knock at the door. It was the sheriff's deputy. He was even shorter than I'd realized, though the hat helped, and he wasn't very old. He was all business, though.

"Sheriff wants to see you and your wife in the dining hall. Right away."

I opened my mouth to say something smart, because that's just how I am, but he'd already turned away and headed back to his car. Probably had an important radio call to make. Tracy and I headed for the grub shack. We were the last ones to get there. While we were going in the door, the Coroner's wagon, a black Chevy panel truck, pulled up the drive and stopped.

Inside the grub shack were the sheriff, the guy with the silver hair I'd figured was the ranch foreman, and some buckaroos I hadn't yet met. Our fellow guests were all assembled, sitting at one of the long tables. Dr. Rumdab looked like he'd just had a very satisfying talk with his lawyer. There was no phone in our cabin, and I didn't figure the other cabins had phones, either. I guessed Rumdab must have insisted on borrowing one of the ranch phones. Tracy and me took seats at the table and nodded to our fellow dudes. Rumdab ignored us and glared at the sheriff, who was standing over by the buffet table.

"Folks, I'm Sheriff Fish" He had a croaky, whiskey voice, "we just wanted to get you all together to let you know what's going on."

He had leathery, tanned skin, and looked about ten years beyond retirement age. These country sheriffs hate giving up their jobs. His eyes were a watery gray, bleached by the sun, and when he took his hat off to scratch his head the ceiling lights bounced off his bald dome.

"I hear," continued Fish, "most of you pulled in this morning, except for a couple of you who arrived last night. Just so you know, not a one of you is under suspicion. We've had a murder—even Clayton County ain't free of them—but we got our ideas about who done it."

Cops always say that. I bet he didn't have a clue.

"As I said, none of you are suspects," droned on the sheriff, "but we'd appreciate it mightily if you just stayed right here on the ranch for a spell. That shouldn't be no trouble. You're all planning to stay here for a few days anyhow. If any of you cares to visit our fine town of Quail Eye, you're welcome to. But don't leave the state, and don't go anywhere without telling us where you're going. I want you all to go ahead and have a wonderful time at the Carefree Buckaroo. You got any questions, now's the time to ask. Let 'er rip!"

"My lawyer assures me you can't detain us," said Rumdab, digging his spurs in.

The sheriff nodded his head. "If you want to listen to your lawyer instead of me, that's your lookout. I don't figure he runs Clayton County, though."

"Who got killed, and how?" I asked. Tracy kicked me under the table.

"An employee of the Carefree Buckaroo. A horse wrangler by the name of Brice Holcombe. Fine fellow, known him for years. I won't give you no particulars, but he was likely strangled with a rope. There were some horse tracks, but they ain't uncommon on a ranch."

"Did this guy have any enemies?" I asked. Tracy elbowed me in the ribs.

"Reckon he had at least one, but Brice was a friendly fellow."

Sissy Dell, sitting on a chair next to the pot-bellied stove in the center of the room, burst into tears. A bandy-legged cowboy with skin like an old boxing glove let out a wail and dragged a bandana out of his jean's pocket to honk his nose into. He shook his head, swept off his hat, and flapped it against his dusty chaps. All the other men in the room who were wearing hats took them off. My fedora was back in our cabin.

"I got nothing more to say," said the sheriff. I noticed he wore a Smith & Wesson thirty-eight on his hip like any regular cop. "You folks are free to start having some fun."

He walked to the door, turned and nodded his head at us, then left.

Breedlaw, the ranch foreman, stepped forward from a corner and addressed us all. He was maybe sixty, with a silver mustache to match his hair. His eyes were squinty and his yellow teeth would have looked at home in the mouth of a mule. He had a drinker's lumpy nose.

"I want to welcome you all to the Carefree Buckaroo. In a minute here, our wrangler — Hawk Luster — will be taking you all to the corral. We've got horses saddled for you, and I hope you're ready to ride. Some of you might not be expert riders. That's perfectly fine. We'll get you in the saddle and make sure you don't fall off your horse. You'll get back to the chuck house in time for a right fine lunch. Since we're getting such a late start, the lunch will be light. We don't want to spoil your appetite for the barbeque we're planning for your supper, courtesy of Sissy Dell and Panhandle. Let me introduce you to the other members of our ranch." He waved a big hand at the bandy-legged nose honker. "This is Sheepy Burdell. Don't let his name fool you. He's a cattleman and horseman down to the bone. Sheepy takes care of our mustangs, including shoeing and doctoring. This fellow here," he gestured at the beauty in black, "is Hawk Luster, our wrangler." Luster bowed to us and smiled bright enough to make the dames want to fan themselves.

"I thought the wrangler got killed," said the willowy guy named Walter.

Breedlaw turned his hat around in his hands. "The ranch needs two wranglers. We got quite a string of horses."

My guess was that Hawk was the ornamental wrangler, while the deceased Brice had done the real work.

"This man standing with his head down—he's a shy one," continued Breedlaw, "is our guide, Drew Kettles." He poked a finger at a young man with reddish hair and a round, pockmarked, face. Kettles looked at all of us and turned red. "Drew knows all the trails around here, and he won't let you get lost. Standing by the kitchen door there is my own wife, Wheezy." A middle-aged woman with a face like Sissy Dell's, only older and without the smile, said howdy to us. "Then there's Audra Tubbs, another guide, who's now circulating the maps to you."

A girl of twenty or so was walking along our table passing out rustic-looking maps of the ranch. She was short and alarmingly curvy, with a vacant smile on her upturned-nosed face.

"That's everyone you need to know on the ranch," said Breedlaw. "We got some other hands—this is a working cattle and horse ranch—

but you likely won't be seeing them. Now, folks, I'm going to turn you over to Hawk. He'll have you riding like real hell-for-leather cowboys and cowgirls in no time. Lunch will be waiting for you when you get back. Bring your appetites."

Hawk rounded us up and moved us out. He herded us over to a big corral next to the barn. I ducked out and went back to our cabin to fetch my fedora and make sure that Eben and Mayhew had food and water. I also made sure I had my snub-nose thirty-eight in my jeans pocket before I raced back to the corral. Hawk was introducing Tracy to a pretty paint named Candy. He took one look at my fedora and frowned. I guess I wasn't dressing the part.

"Candy won't bite. ma'am," Hawk said to Tracy. "She's mighty friendly."

"I grew up on a ranch," Tracy told him. "I know which end of a horse eats and which one doesn't."

I noticed she was wearing her glasses for a change. I imagine she wanted to see all there was to look at on the dude ranch. Or maybe she just wanted to get a good gander at Hawk. She climbed into the saddle like an old hand and looked around at the other dudes with a smirk on her face. She was one of those girls who look good in glasses. The "ranch" she'd grown up on had maybe a dozen cattle and two horses, but I guess she'd at least learned how to ride.

"I've got just the horse for your husband here,"

Hawk told her. He turned to me and flashed a crooked smile. "Old Lucky is as gentle as a dove. I'll get him for you."

I was suspicious. I knew the kind of tricks cowboys played on dudes. I half expected Lucky to be a fish-tailing rodeo bronc. Hawk led a big dappled gray over to me. It's eyes looked sleepy. I wasn't fooled.

"You always mount on the left side," the lovely Hawk told me. Hell, even I knew that. I'd seen Westerns, and the farm in Kansas where I'd grown up had an out-sized horse named Pedro that I'd ridden plenty of times.

"That so?" I asked. "Even in England? I know they drive on the wrong side of the street there."

"We ain't in England," said Hawk. "Put your foot in the stirrup and climb on up. I'll hold Lucky's bridle for you."

I got onto Lucky's back without any trouble. He stood still, twitching one ear. He smelled like a horse.

"Now," said Hawk, "what Lucky likes, just to get him started, is for you to nudge him with your heels."

Here it comes, I thought. Axe is going over Lucky's ears. But I was too stubborn to make my suspicions known to Hawk. I touched my heels to the bronc's flanks. Lucky whirled around and jumped about twenty feet in the air. I stayed in the saddle. He came down on stiff legs and danced around like he was at a sock hop. He bucked and twisted and had all kinds of fun. I ended up on the ground. Hawk helped me to my feet and settled down Lucky.

"I don't rightly understand it," Hawk apologized, with a poker face. "A fly must have been bothering him. You want to try again?"

"Sure, let me at him."

Hawk held the horse and I crawled back into the saddle. I barely grazed Lucky's flanks with my heels. He went off like a roman candle and I was reintroduced to the dirt. I banged my head. That made me mad. I'd already been hit in the head with a flashlight, and now a horse was beating me up. Hawk offered me a hand and I knocked it away. I headed for Lucky.

"Whoa! Whoa! That's enough," said Hawk. He started laughing. He turned to the other dudes. "Here at the Carefree Buckaroo we like to have our little jokes. Ain't nobody can ride Lucky, not even me. You can saddle him, and sit on him, but he won't be rode." He turned to me. "You did good. Most dudes fall off sooner."

I looked at my fellow dudes. Half of them were laughing and the other half looked horrified.

"I'm fine," I told them, slapping the dust off my clothes.

"No hard feelings?" asked Hawk, laying his pretty hand on my shoulder.

"No, just bruises. Quite the joke."

"I got some hard feelings," said Tracy, coming forward and getting in Hawk's face. "That was mean! My husband could have been hurt! This is our honeymoon."

"Ma'am, I'm awful sorry. I don't know what got into me."

While they were talking I walked over to Lucky. I climbed back into the saddle. Tracy rushed over and grabbed my stirrup.

"Get down! Don't be an idiot!" She turned to the other dudes. "He's hurt. He's a detective. Night before last a tough guy sapped him in the head, three times. If he wasn't as tough as he is, he would have been killed. On top of that, some ape waylaid Axe in his office and threw some slugs at his head."

"Ugh!" said curly-haired Mabel. "Slugs! I hate them. We have them in our garden."

"I didn't realize you were injured," said Hawk, coming over and grabbing Lucky's bridle. "Get on down. I'm sorry. I'll get you a good horse."

I stayed where I was. I was getting ready to dig my heels into the horse, but Tracy gave me a look.

"I don't want to be a widow," she said. "Quit showing off. Get down."

If it hadn't been our honeymoon, I wouldn't have listened to her. I got down.

"You sure nobody can ride this horse?" Tracy asked Hawk.

"Nobody ever has, ma'am."

"You'd be willing to bet money?"

"I'd give twenty dollars to the man who could stay on that horse for five minutes."

"What about a woman?" Tracy asked, and before anybody could stop her she jumped into Lucky's saddle, grabbed the reins, and swatted the horse with her silly cowboy hat.

The horse jumped the corral fence. Tracy stuck to its back like a molasses-soaked thistle. Lucky jumped and dived and squirmed and got all lathered up. But he couldn't shake my wife. Tracy hung on like a Gila monster with a mouthful of prospector. The saddle finally pulled loose and Tracy and it landed on a nice grassy spot. I ran over to her.

"You OK? What got into you?"

"Look who's talking. I'm fine. I landed on my caboose." She walked back to the corral and looked Hawk in the eye. "Was I on five minutes?"

"Ma'am, I reckon you were. I don't have twenty dollars on me now, but I'll pay you in the morning. Will that be all right?"

"Sure. Nobody's going to let you forget. When I was a kid in 4H, I had the meanest horse this side of Mars." She turned and looked off into the distance. "I think Lucky's going to be gone for a while."

I noticed her glasses weren't on her face. Damn it! She never wore the things and now she'd worn them to ride a rodeo monster. I looked around on the ground and found the glasses. Amazingly, they weren't broken. I walked over and handed them to her, shaking my head.

"You could have gotten yourself killed, potato

head," I said.

"That's my line, skunk cabbage."

When you meet a swell girl like Tracy, you'd be a fool not to marry her.

The show was over. Hawk picked out horses for all of us, including one for me. My new horse was an old buckskin named Butter. He looked at me with come-hither eyes and almost begged me to ride him. Hawk arranged us in single file and led us up a long crooked trail that led into some nice hills. The joke he'd played on me had lowered him in the opinion of the dames. I could tell by the way they looked at him. But he did his best to make up for it. He put me right behind him in the line. He'd picked up my hat—Lucky had stepped on it—from the corral dirt and returned it to me.

"You got some sand, mister," he told me, loud enough for everyone to hear.

Walter, the sulky guy married to Betsy, called out to Hawk.

"Don't be playing anymore of those tricks, Cowboy," he said. "I didn't come up here to get my neck broken."

"I just hope my horse likes me," said Mabel, with a nervous giggle.

When we'd been riding for half an hour or so, Hawk started singing. His voice was a smoky baritone, and he sang about dusky-eyed senoritas, and grim-lipped lawmen. By the time he was through, he'd gained back the admiration of the damsels. We stopped in an open area where a space had been cleared of rocks and grass and cactus. There was a split-rail fence nearby, and Hawk had us tie up our cayuses. He opened up his saddle bags and brought out half-a-dozen glass globes about the size of baseballs.

"I'm fixing to put on a little shooting exhibition," he told us.

He laid out the glass balls on the ground and drew his revolver and twirled it and threw it in the air and caught it. I noticed he'd switched guns from the first time I'd seen him. Instead of the fancy pearl-handled Colt he'd worn before, this new gun had a longer barrel and wood grips. It looked worn and well-used.

He tossed one of the balls about twenty feet in the air and shot it to pieces when it reached its zenith. He did the same thing with the other glass globes. It was impressive, but I knew the trick. The gun was a special one for showmen, invented when Wild West shows were still popular. I was sure of it. No doubt Hawk's revolver had a smooth bore, like a shotgun, and the cartridges were loaded with sand. When he fired off a shot, the sand spread out a couple of feet and blasted the glass balls to pieces. It was a lot easier than using regular bullets. But it looked good, and we all ooed and ahed. Except for me, but I'm just a sour old gumshoe.

We got back on our mounts and rode through some pretty country with stands of pine, with the breeze blowing through them, and tinkling streams of clear water, and plenty of big rocks and boulders to look at. Then we turned and headed back to the ranch and our lunch. None of us fell off our horses.

6

It's hard to talk to folks when you're riding single file. Maybe when we got back to the grub house I'd be able to chew the fat with my fellow dudes and the ranch hands. I wanted to get to know everybody so I could make a guess as to who might be the best suspect for Brice Holcombe's murder. Every dude except for me and Tracy had arrived this morning, but that didn't mean they couldn't have snuck up the night before and strangled the cowpoke. That thought actually seemed kind of silly to me. Maybe I was already missing working on a case instead of playing cowpoke. Still, I wanted to talk to Panhandle. I wanted to get his side of things before I called his aunt and told her where her DeSoto was. I just hoped Tracy didn't catch on to what I was doing. Hell, I can't help it. I'm a nosey guy!

We got the horses back to the corral. All the dudes filed down to the pump behind the cabins to wash the trail dust off their paws and mugs before lunch. I didn't like that the outhouses were so close to the pump, but the water tasted OK. Then we went to the chow house and Sissy Dell led us out back to a grassy place with picnic tables, a native stone barbeque apparatus, a croquet lawn, and horseshoe-throwing pits. There was even a little concrete shuffleboard area. Panhandle was busy burning burgers. I told Tracy to pick a spot for us at one of the tables, then I moseyed over to Panhandle.

"Howdy Panhandle!" I greeted him. "You remind me of a guy named Billy. Ever hear of him? Nice ride, by the way."

Panhandle flinched, but recovered his cowboy stoicism quick enough.

"Why, if it ain't my cousin Miles. Or is it Axe?"

"Axe. What are we having for grub? Rabbit?"

"That was Ned that took the rabbit. Me, I'm innocent. What are you, a peeper?"

"Good guess."

"I knew you weren't no lost cousin. Aunt Aggie can't fool us that easy."

"Sure, I did a job for her. She wanted me to stick around and recover her car for her, but I was otherwise engaged."

"Engaged? I thought you was married." He laughed a big horse laugh. "Listen, I can explain about the car."

"You mean you can tell me how you stole the battery first, and then the rest of the DeSoto?"

"It wasn't like that. Honest. Before you and

Auntie took off to rescue Percy, I was waiting for a phone call from the ranch. When I got the call, I had an errand to run. I needed to get some cash to my bookie. I like the dogs and the horses. That pickup that Ned and me own wouldn't start. I couldn't even crank start it. The damned jalopy doesn't run half the time."

"So you decided to take Miss Weatherby's car to get to your bookie," I said.

"Yeah, that's how it was. But the damned DeSoto wouldn't start either. I popped the hood and found the battery gone."

"Neighborhood hoodlums?"

"Naw. I'm guessing it was Ned. He snuck out in the night and kiped the battery to get even with Auntie for wanting to burn his feet. So, anyway, I thumbed a ride to the gas station and bought a new battery."

"Very kind of you."

"Don't get smart. That's how it was. One of the grease monkeys gave me a ride back and I put in the new battery, then went over to see Sal, my bookie. I haven't heard yet if I won. Twenty smackers on Pogo Stick, a long shot."

"Is that a horse or a dog?" I asked.

"A pony. Who'd name a dog Pogo Stick?"

"Sure. I should have guessed that. Then what happened?"

"I waited around for you and Auntie to get back. You sure took your sweet time. What were you doing, necking in the woods?"

STEVEN LEROY NELSON

"None of your business."

"I waited as long as I could, but I needed to get to the Carefree Buckaroo. So I ended up borrowing the DeSoto."

"Sure. I'm tempted to call your aunt and tell her where her car is."

"She already knows. I left her a note on the little table next to the front door. She always looks there. She'll likely send the girls up here to fetch the car."

I thought about it. The story actually made some sense. But none of it explained where he got the money for his fancy duds. Maybe he'd been dipping into Aunt Aggie's purse.

"How'd you end up so flush?" I asked.

"I've been saving up. I do pretty well with the doggies sometimes."

"You didn't tell your aunt, or the others, that you were going to be working up here?"

"Naw. They'd do something to screw things up. That's just how they are."

"OK. Get back to your barbequing. Don't burn my burger."

"Which one's yours?"

"The one that's not burnt."

I joined Tracy at the table. Walter and Betsy sat across from us. Walter seemed sulky. Betsy was friendly. Maybe too friendly. She kept giving me the eye. What kind of dame turns on the charm for a mug like me?

"Where are you folks from?" Tracy asked them.

"Back East," said Walter.

"Any particular state?" I asked.

"We move around a lot."

"We're living in Jersey," Betsy volunteered. "Walter has a restless foot, though. We'll be moving to Pennsylvania pretty soon."

"What do you do, Walter?" I asked.

"He's an inventor," said Betsy.

"I work in a warehouse," said Walter.

"Sure, he's working in a warehouse now, but he's just getting started as an inventor. He's working on a bread toaster that's powered by water. You hook it up to your kitchen faucet."

"I don't see how that would work," said Tracy, frowning.

"It doesn't," said Walter. "It's a flop, a failure, like everything else I come up with."

"He's just being modest," Betsy gushed. "Tell these nice people about the cigarette filter you invented. It's made out of ground glass."

"It stinks," said Walter. "Nobody wants it, none of the cigarette makers. I'm a lousy inventor."

"Someday Walter will be rich and famous," said Betsy.

"We'll die in the gutter," sighed Walter. "I'm a loser." He took a long swig from a bottle of beer and shook his head sadly.

"What do you do, Betsy?" asked Tracy. "Any kids?"

"No, not yet. I work at the Woolworths."

"We can't afford kids," said Walter. "And

Betsy's got to work because of me."

Betsy gave me a big smile and winked. I don't know how Tracy didn't notice.

Sissy Dell and Panhandle started bringing trays of food over to the tables. The chow was pretty good, even if Panhandle had burned some of the meat. I had two hamburgers and two barbeque sandwiches, a ton of potato salad, and a field's worth of corn on the cob. And this was the ranch's idea of a light lunch. I was ready for a nap. When they brought out the ice cream, I sneered.

"Axe doesn't like ice cream," explained Tracy. "Isn't that crazy?"

"I thought everybody loved ice cream," said Betsy.

"I invented a new kind of ice cream maker," said Walter. "Diesel. Everybody hated it. Lost money on it."

"This ice cream is great," said Betsy. She made calf eyes at me. "Won't you try just a bite, Axe? I'll make choo-choo noises."

"I had a bad experience as a child," I said. "I found a frozen baby rat in a hot fudge sundae."

"He's lying," said Tracy. She's always spoiling things for me.

"I invented a new rat poison once," said Walter. "It made them grow. They loved the stuff."

"Why don't you tell them about all your successful inventions, dear?" Betsy asked him.

"Honey, there haven't been any."

"Like I said, he's modest," said Betsy. She

caught my eye and pouted her mouth.

"What are we doing after lunch, I wonder?" asked Tracy.

"Sleeping, I hope," I said.

"I heard we were going for a walk," said Betsy. "Up to the big ranch house where the owner lives. I guess it's something to see."

"Primus Roan is the rancher's name," said Tracy. She had strawberry ice cream all over her mouth. I didn't kiss it off. "He's Panhandle's great uncle, I think."

About the time we were through eating, the bandy-legged guy named Sheepy Burdell made an appearance.

"Folks," he told us, "I reckon you're about stuffed with Sissy Dell and Panhandle's fine lunch. We're going to help you with that by taking you all for a walk. It'll help your digestion and work the kinks out of your joints from riding. You'll all be the better for it. You finish up now and we'll get going."

There were some groans from some of the diners, but everybody got up and we followed Sheepy. He took us out onto the main road and we started hiking up it. Sheepy's bowed legs made it hard for him to get up speed, and that was fine with the rest of us. Since we weren't on a narrow trail and forced to go single-file, we strung out along the road in little groups. I took Tracy's arm and guided her over to where Dr. Rumdab and Lilly were walking side by side.

"I want to talk to these folks," I whispered to Tracy.

"No murder talk," she whispered back. "Say, what's with you and the hussy?"

"Who, Betsy? I didn't think you noticed. I don't know what's up with her. Maybe she wants to ditch laugh-a-minute Walter. I didn't encourage her. I ignored every one of her amorous glances."

"Just make sure you keep that up. I think the doctor's a sourpuss."

"Let's find out."

We caught up with the doctor and his wife.

"We're Tracy and Axe," Tracy introduced us.

"I'm Lilly, and this is my husband, Karl."

Karl gave us a curt nod. He had something gray on his upper lip. I think it was supposed to be a mustache. Lilly was heavily made-up, but she couldn't have been much past thirty. I wondered if Karl was a baby doctor and had robbed one of the cradles. Lilly was a peach, pretty and vivacious. Karl was an old stick with indigestion.

"This trip was my wife's idea," he told us. "I wanted to go to a spa in Zurich."

"You can go to a spa anytime, dear," said Lilly. "Riding horses and eating beans will do a lot more for you than going to an old spa and soaking in smelly water."

"I didn't realize I required improvement," Karl grumbled.

Lilly turned to us and stage whispered. "He's just upset about the murder."

"We might be next, you know," said Karl.

"There isn't likely to be any more killings," I said, as if I knew what I was talking about.

"Is that so?" asked Karl, twitching his little mustache. "How is it that you know this?"

"My husband's a detective," said Tracy.

"Oh, that's right," said Rumdab. "I believe you brought that up at the corral." He turned to me. "How are you feeling, by the way? You took some terrible tumbles."

"I'm all right. I've got some sore ribs and a bruised shoulder. What kind of a doc are you?"

"A general practitioner, to my infinite regret. I should have become a specialist, or a pathologist."

"Karl's bedside manner could use some work," said Lilly, laughing. She had one of those laughs that seem more like a seizure.

"Great lunch, huh?" said Tracy.

"I'll say," said Lilly, rubbing her stomach.

"It was entirely unhealthy," said Karl. "We'll have to engage in a strict diet and exercise regime when we return home."

"Don't be a wet blanket, honey, you know you loved that barbeque."

"I admit that it was appetizing," said Karl.

Sheepy stopped us and pointed to a driveway at one side of the road. He led us up it. Some of the dudes were starting to puff and pant. Flat-landers!

"This here's the house," said Sheepy, after we'd walked about half a mile.

It was a log-built monstrosity, two-stories high, with twin towers and a wealth of windows, but it might have been too small to hold dog races in. I wondered if Primus Roan lived alone. There was a barn and corral on one side, and a stream—with a bridge—roiled along the front. The dudes, including me, were impressed.

"Mr. Roan is laid up now," Sheepy said. "He got throwed by a stallion some years back. The Roans have made most of their money off of raising and breeding horses. Hop-A-Long Cassidy rode a horse from this ranch in some of his movies. And there's been some mighty fine race horses bred here."

"Was Lucky bred here?" I asked.

"Lucky? Why, yes, he was. They don't always turn out good. You folks can take pictures if you want."

"Can we go inside?" asked Mabel, the hardware guy's wife.

"No, ma'am, I'm sorry. Mr. Roan favors privacy."

Some of us took pictures. Tracy tried out the new Brownie she'd bought for the trip. Then we turned around and headed back to the dude ranch. Some of us were getting pretty footsore.

"Folks," said Sheepy, when we were once again standing in front of the dining hall, "there's horseshoe-pitching and croquet out back, or you might want to start up a card game. But some of you might want to take naps."

"That's for me," said Tracy, winking at me.

"I might actually want to sleep," I said.

"I knew I should have married a younger guy."

We went back to our cabin and played with the cats. They were awfully happy to see us. In our absence they'd managed to pull down the window curtain, unpack one of our suitcases, and overturn their water dish. Sheepy had told us that supper wouldn't be until seven since we'd gotten off to a late start that morning.

"What do you think of our fellow dudes?" Tracy asked.

"Hard to say. I haven't really talked to Curt and Mabel yet. The doc's not as bad as I thought he was, and his wife's swell."

"I wish I could think of a way to cheer up Walter."

"You'd think being married to Betsy would make him happy," I said, with a leer.

"You stay away from her. She's not part of our honeymoon plans."

"I wonder which one of us dudes could be a murderer."

"Don't start that talk. Besides, the sheriff thinks one of the ranch employees did it."

"He was just talking. I'm sure he's looking into all of our backgrounds, especially yours. He's got our registration information. I'm going to talk to Panhandle about the killing."

"No sleuthing on our honeymoon. Come kiss me instead."

"Sure. Do we have anything to drink around here?"

"I've got two bottles of champagne in our suitcase, but it's warm."

"We could take a blanket and a couple of glasses and go find a stream to cool the bottles in."

"How romantic. Should we take the cats?"

"We'll take them out for a romp later."

We gathered up our blanket, a couple of wine glasses Tracy had carefully packed, and the champagne, and headed outside. Mabel Halsey was just coming out the door of the cabin next to ours. Apparently the Halsey's were our neighbors.

"I need to change my shoes," she told us. "How does anybody walk in cowboy boots?"

"That's why cowboys ride horses," I said.

"What's with the bottles and the blanket? Are you guys going out into the woods? I wouldn't. I mean, I heard you were newlyweds and all, but what about the killer? I didn't even like walking to the cabin by myself, but Curt was busy playing horseshoes. I think he and Panhandle are playing for money."

"You think the killer is waiting out in the woods for his next victim?" Tracy asked her.

Mabel shrugged. "Who knows? I'm not taking any chances."

Tracy gave me a sorrowful look.

"I don't think there's going to be a second murder," I said. "I think it had something to do with the folks who work for the dude ranch. Something personal. We aren't dealing with some kind of crazed killer."

"It'd be a shame to spoil your honeymoon by getting strangled to death," said Mabel.

"I think she's right," Tracy told me. "It's not worth the risk. We can drink our champagne later. Maybe we can use the fridge in the dining hall kitchen to get it nice and cold for us. We can take it back to our cabin with us after supper. What do you say, Axe?"

I had to admit it was the sensible thing to do. "OK, you girls win. We'll play it safe."

"Come join the other dudes," Mabel invited. She didn't have enough nose to sound nasal, but she managed it anyway. "The doctor and his wife are napping, but the rest of us are over behind the dining hall. Betsy and Walter are playing croquet. There's lemonade and iced tea."

"No coffee?" I asked.

"It's too hot for coffee, but maybe Sissy Dell will make some for you if you ask."

Tracy put the blanket and glasses back in our cabin, and we strolled over to the chuck house with Mabel. Mabel was limping a little. We joined the others and I asked Sissy Dell if she had room in the fridge for our champagne.

"Sure we do. You having a little celebration later?"

"You might call it that," I said. "Say, would you mind making me some coffee?"

"Kind of hot for coffee, isn't it? But, sure, if

that's what you want." .

She took the bottles and disappeared into the grub house. I walked over to where Panhandle and Curt were standing near a horseshoe pit. Curt was handing Panhandle some cash.

"Were you playing with marked horseshoes?" I asked Panhandle, when Curt walked away shaking his head.

"Huh? Sure, very funny."

"I want to talk to you about the murder."

"Why me? Talk to Breedlaw."

"He's the foreman. He won't tell me anything, but maybe you will. Any rumors going around in the bunkhouse?"

"Naw. I've learned a thing or two, but I can't talk about it now. I've got these dudes to watch. They're a lot like cows; they don't have much sense. And I've got to start cooking again pretty soon. We can jaw after supper. How's that?"

"Fine, but don't forget. Where's the rest of the Buckaroo crew?"

"Busy. Sheepy's with the horses. Audra's cleaning some of the cabins. Drew's sawing up firewood—we use up a lot of it. Hawk's likely off somewhere looking in the mirror or shining his boots. Care for a game of horseshoes?"

"I thought you said you had to watch the dudes. I think I'll go over and see what my wife's doing."

"You're a lucky guy. Your misses is a looker."

"Tracy? Sure, she's OK. Don't get any ideas."

"Me?" He raised his eyebrows and tried looking innocent.

"Maybe you and Sissy Dell can get together."

"Naw," said Panhandle. "She's prime stock. I don't have a chance. I'm thinking Audra might be worth a try."

"Good luck."

Tracy was off to one side of the croquet lawn — a big oval of mown native grass with wickets — looking at some cactus.

"Lose something?" I asked her.

"The cutest little rattlesnake you ever saw. Only about two feet long. I'm going to catch it for you."

"Thanks, sister." Tracy knows snakes give me the willies. "I don't think you're allowed to capture the wildlife. Come on, I'll buy you a lemonade."

"You're ruining my fun."

"I'm trying to keep you from ruining mine. Leave that poor snake alone. Aren't you afraid of getting bitten?"

"I've got a way with snakes."

"Lucky you. You're starting to sweat. Let's get you out of the sun."

On our way to the roofed veranda in back of the grub shack, I stopped to warn Curt and Mabel about the rattler.

"Tracy just saw a rattlesnake. I'd advise you to give up your croquet game."

Mabel let out a little scream. "You win, Curt. I'm going back to the porch."

Curt gathered up the croquet mallets and the colored balls and followed his wife. He stopped to talk to me a minute.

"First a murder, now a rattlesnake," he said. "A man hates to think he won't survive his own vacation." He had a buzz cut which only made his fat face look fatter. "Makes me want to take up smoking again. I quit. Doctor's orders."

"Doctors just don't want any of us to have a good time."

"I'll say. Mine wants me to lose weight, too. I might as well die and get it over with."

7

We joined the others under the porch roof. There were some rustic wooden chairs and a couple of love seats. They looked kind of splintery. Tracy was talking to Betsy. I wondered if she was giving her an earful about having made eyes at me at lunch. I hoped there wasn't going to be a cat fight. Walter was sitting in one of the chairs, staring off at the sky. He looked like his favorite pony had just died. I sidled over to Tracy and Betsy.

"I got my own lemonade," Tracy told me. She was holding a misty glass. "Sissy Dell says your coffee is ready."

"Thanks."

Betsy goggled at me. "So, you're a real detective? Tracy says you're the best. I'm so glad you're here. Maybe you can figure out who killed that poor wrangler."

"I'll leave that to the sheriff. We're on our honeymoon, and my new bride has forbidden me to do any gumshoe work."

"But you might be able to figure things out," said Betsy. She gave me a smile that almost knocked me down.

"I'm sure that Sheriff Fish will have the whole case wrapped up in no time," I said.

Doc Rumdab and Lilly came around the corner and joined us.

"Grab some lemonade or iced tea," Sissy Dell told them, coming back out of the grub house. She brought a tin cup of coffee over to me. "I don't know how you take it. Can I get you cream or sugar?"

"Thanks, no. I drink it black."

"Do you have mineral water?" asked the doc.

"We have spring water, from our own well."

"I suppose that will have to do. Thank you. Is there a chess set on the ranch I can borrow?"

"We've got checkers, both American and Chinese."

Rumdab make a face.

"I don't like playing chess with you anyway, Karl," said Lilly. "You never let me win."

"Tracy saw a rattlesnake," Mabel told the newcomers. She turned to Tracy. "How big was it?"

"Not more than eight feet." Tracy grinned at Mabel's shocked expression. "No, it was just a baby, pinkish gray, with only three or four rattles. A really cute snake."

Mabel squealed and ran to Curt for protection.

We spent the next couple of hours chatting and playing games and relaxing. Then Panhandle announced that our grub was ready.

He and Sissy Dell put on another good spread: barbequed chicken and homemade biscuits. Fried potatoes and coleslaw. Apple pie and cherry pie for dessert. They even brought out an ice chest full of beer, but I stuck with my coffee. After we'd eaten, Panhandle unlimbered his guitar and Sissy Dell sang us a bunch of cowboy songs. When the beer was depleted and the serenade was over, the dudes scattered and headed for their cabins. I buttonholed Panhandle and reminded him we needed to talk.

"Sure," he said, "but not yet. I got to help clean up. Wait out here; I'll be through in a jiffy."

Tracy wanted to know what was going on. I didn't want to tell her but I did.

"Panhandle's going to tell me what he knows about Holcombe getting killed."

"You promised to leave your detective hat at home."

"I know, but I wasn't counting on anyone getting murdered. I just want to talk to Panhandle, that's all."

"Then I'm going to talk to him too."

"Fine."

The night was turning out nice. The air was chilly but sweet and fresh. We could hear some frogs down by the creek, and there were some crickets, but not many. There was a yellow moon rising in the sky, and big clusters of stars. I counted them. In about twenty minutes Panhandle came out the back door and joined me and Tracy.

"Great supper," Tracy told him. "Who taught you to cook?"

"My mom. She was kind of sickly, and us kids had to learn to fend for ourselves. I was cooking before I was out of knee pants."

"You wore knee pants?" I asked.

"Just an expression, Mr. Detective."

"Tell us what you know about Brice Holcombe's death," I said.

"Sure. I didn't really know him. He wasn't working here when I was here before. The reason I left the Carefree Buckaroo was because of a couple of murders that happened up here."

"Jeez," I said. "What kind of place is this?"

"Yeah," said Tracy, "It's supposed to be a nice friendly dude ranch."

"It is," said Panhandle. "The murders didn't have nothing to do with the dudes. Two years ago it was a trail guide and another wrangler that got killed. Same way. They were lassoed and strangled. After the second murder folks started calling the killer Jack the Roper. Funny, huh?"

"Sure," I said. "Hilarious. So now Jack the Roper's back."

"I don't think so," said Panhandle, "for two reasons. One, Brice Holcombe was strangled with a rope right enough, but the knot was wrong. The lasso was tied with a plain slip knot, not a Honda knot."

"What the hell is a Honda knot?" I asked.

"Something every cowboy knows how to tie. A special kind of slipknot. If I had a rope I could show you."

"That's OK. So you're saying the guy who killed Holcombe isn't the same guy who committed the murders two years ago. But he wants to look like he's Jack the Roper. A copycat murder."

"That's what I figure," said Panhandle, scratching an armpit. "I talked to Breedlaw after the sheriff was here. The sheriff thinks it's a different killer."

"All right," broke in Tracy. "What's your second reason for thinking it's a different killer this time?"

"I think the killer from last time is dead. I think I know who it was."

"Really?" I asked. "The cops caught him?"

"No. He died. It was likely Old Man Juniper. Ezra Juniper. He owned the Lazy Circle Ranch, which borders the Carefree Buckaroo. For years, old Ezra made the claim that there was a spring-head that belonged to him and not the Buckaroo. He said the boundaries hadn't been marked off right. I think the old man was crazy. He tried to get Primus Roan to turn the spring over to him."

"What's the big deal?" asked Tracy. "It's just some water."

"Hawk told me you grew up on a ranch," said Panhandle. "Is that so?"

"Yes, a little ranch, near Quartz Quarry. The Lucky Clover. That's my family's name. Clover."

"You had plenty of water?"

"I'll say. The house used to flood about every other year. A big stream runs through the place."

"OK," said Panhandle. "Up here things are different. We got some little trickles for streams and not much else. Water's a big deal in these parts. Some ranchers would kill for more water."

"Like Old Man Juniper," I said.

"That's right. He sicced the law on Mr. Roan, my great-uncle. But it got him nowhere. So then he started making threats. He killed some of the Buckaroo's cattle, and had a couple of punchers beat up. Mr. Roan didn't budge. That's when Jack the Roper showed up. I think Ezra Juniper was behind the killings. In fact, I think he was the Roper. He was old, but a cowboy's as good as the horse he rides."

"He was never arrested?" I asked.

"Naw. They couldn't find enough evidence. Juniper had a couple of strokes. The second one ended up killing him. And Jack the Roper disappeared."

"What did Primus Roan think about it?"

"I think he always believed Juniper was the killer."

"That was two years ago?" I asked. "Do you have any idea who this new killer might be?"

"No, but he ain't a cowboy. The knot proves that. Somebody had it in for Holcombe, I figure. They killed him and covered their tracks by making it look like the Roper did it."

"So," said Tracy, "somebody local. Not one of the dudes."

"Looks like."

"You could have done it yourself, Panhandle," I said.

"Why would I?"

"Maybe you wanted Holcomb's job. You knew the story about the Roper."

"Sure, but I didn't do it. I'm a cook, not a wrangler. I couldn't have gotten Brice's job. Besides, I know how to tie a Honda knot."

"You were likely in on the rabbit-napping with Ned. You stole your aunt's car. You could be a killer."

"I ain't. And I didn't take the bunny neither. I didn't steal Auntie's car. I borrowed it. Hell, I might be lazy, but I ain't a crook."

"Whatever you say. Who do you think killed the wrangler?"

Panhandle shrugged and raised his shaggy eyebrows. The light from the porch just barely reached us and most of his face was in shadow. "How would I know? I'd guess it was somebody from town, some guy who didn't care much for Brice."

"What about the dudes? One of them could have done it," said Tracy.

"They're mostly from out of state. None of them could know the guy. Why would they kill him?" asked Panhandle.

"You got a point," I said. "But don't be so sure

none of us didn't know the dead guy. One of us could have known him in the past, maybe hated him, and chose their vacation spot here so they could send Brice out of this vale of tears. That's just the kind of a world that we live in, Tracy. I hate to blot out your sunny illusions."

"You enjoy doing that. None of us dudes would know about the Roper," said Tracy.

"They could have heard the story," I said. "They might have talked to somebody at the ranch when they were making their reservations. I wouldn't take any of the dudes off the suspect list yet."

It was getting late. Panhandle wanted to head for the bunkhouse. He fetched our now cold bottles of champagne and me and Tracy headed for our cabin. We spread our blanket out in front of the cabin and brought the cats outside. For the next hour or so we drank champagne, looked at the stars, and retrieved Eben and Mayhew every time they strayed too far.

"The killer slipped up when he tied the wrong kind of knot in the lariat," I said. I couldn't stop thinking about the murder.

"We didn't slip up when we tied the knot," said Tracy, cuddling up to me.

"We sure didn't, precious." I pulled her closer and kissed her.

In a while we rounded up our wild boys — they loved it outside and puffed up like dandelions — and went into the cabin.

8

Breakfast was at seven. The mountain air gave us all appetites. We stuffed ourselves with pancakes, eggs and bacon, toast, orange juice, and coffee. After we'd eaten, the two guides, Audra and Drew, made their appearance and gave us the day's schedule. They both stood before us and gave us our instructions.

"Cowboys and cowgirls," said Audra, in her thin, high-pitched voice, "we're taking you on another horseback ride this morning. It'll be longer than yesterday's. We're taking lunch along with us. We're headed up into the mountains. The trail is steep and it's important that everybody stay on the trail. We don't want anyone getting lost or hurt. I'll be leading, and Drew will be eating our dust in the rear. You'll have the same mounts as yesterday unless someone has a problem with that."

None of us spoke. We liked our horses just fine. Drew took over the talking. His voice squeaked, and his pimply face turned red.

"Dudes, it's important you stay in your saddles. Keep your feet in the stirrups at all times. When we get to the steeper parts of the trail I want you should lean forward in your saddles and hang on-to the horns if you have to. We may be seeing some wildlife, maybe even a bear or two. You can take pictures, but don't go waving your arms or hats. And don't throw sandwiches or other chuck at the animals. They'll just want more, and then they'll come and eat one of us. Don't let your horses graze while you're riding. Keep their heads up. They'll get plenty to eat once they're back in the barn. If you need to fetch anything from your cabins, now's the time. I recommend hats and sun tan lotion. The sun up here is fierce on account of the thin air."

Sheepy had our horses saddled and ready at the corral. There were also a couple of pack mules loaded up with our lunch. Audra led us up a dif-ferent trail from yesterday's, and pretty soon we were climbing through stands of spruce and pine. Drew and the pack mules took up the rear. By the time the sun got high in the sky I was getting sleepy. Old Butter seemed to be nodding off too. I had to keep nudging him with my heels to keep him from stopping. At one point, we saw a bear, kind of cinnamon-colored and big. He was eating berries off of some bushes. Audra stopped us all.

"That be a black bear, even though it ain't black," she told us. "We're safe enough. He wants berries more than he wants us. I'd get your cameras out if I was you."

Drew rode up with us and I noticed he had a saddle rifle in a scabbard along with a six-shooter on his gun belt.

"I don't want nobody to get no closer to that bear," he told us. "Just stay in your saddles and take some nice pictures to show the folks back home."

All the dudes got excited and snapped pictures and chattered like chipmunks. A little farther up the trail we spotted some deer, then a marmot on a rock, and some hawks sailing in the sky. Then we rode out into a high meadow and came across some grazing white-faced cattle. At one end of the meadow was a split-rail fence and some rustic picnic tables. A little stream snaked along in lazy curves and trilled and rippled on the rocks. We got off our broncs and tied them to the fence and got ready for lunch. There were big juicy sandwiches, and sliced fruit, and lemonade and iced tea, but no coffee. There were some kind of fritters for dessert. We sat in the sun and ate and drank and talked about the animals we'd seen. It was a beautiful day and a beautiful place.

"Don't you wish we could stay here forever?" Tracy asked me.

"It'd be tough finding work."

"I think I'd like a job at a dude ranch. If not the Carefree Buckaroo, then a different one."

"I'd miss being a detective."

"You'd miss getting knocked on the head and shot at?"

"Yeah, I'm used to it. It reminds me of my childhood."

"Maybe you could get a job as a sheriff's deputy."

"No thanks. They're just cops with cowboy hats. I don't get along with cops."

"You have two cops for friends," said Tracy.

"Sure, but Blythe and Biff are different. They're almost like actual people."

Some clouds were coming in and it looked like it might rain. A chill breeze was fussing with our hats.

"Folks," Drew said, "we need to get back to the ranch. I don't want I should scare you, but lightning storms up here ain't a bucket of fun. We got slickers for you all if it comes to rain."

Lightning was a lot scarier than bears. Drew and Audra packed the remains of our lunch onto the mules and got us back on our horses. On the way down, the two guides horse-whipped us into learning trail songs and trying to sing them. Not one of us could sing for beans except Tracy. She sang on key, and she had a lot of lung power. I'd never heard her sing before.

"Is there anything you can't do?" I asked her.

"Yes. I can't leave you. Ever."

"Sounds swell to me. If you ever left me, I'd have to track you down."

"At least you're in the right profession."

When we got back to the ranch, Audra addressed us.

"Did all of you have fun?" she asked. We all cheered. "Tonight's supper is going to be an hour early. Six. We're having a square dance in the dining hall. Dress up in your best. Sheepy plays a mean fiddle, so get ready to do-si-do."

"I never asked you," Tracy said to me, "can you dance?" We were standing a little apart from the others.

"I can cut a rug pretty good. At gun point."

"So I'll bring a shotgun to the dance. Anyway, I'll need one to keep Betsy away from you."

"I thought you decided she was OK."

"Sure. I think she makes eyes at all the guys. But she needs to make you the exception."

"Folks," Drew called out to us. "Same as yesterday, this is your time to play games or take a nap if you want. If any of you wants to shake the saddle creaks out of your bones, you're welcome to take a walk. Just make sure you stay on the trails."

"Especially with that murderer around," said Doc Rumdab. The guy was a spoil sport. Everybody grew quiet.

"I hear the sheriff made an arrest," said Drew. "It's likely the man who killed poor Brice is behind bars. Don't let it worry you none. You're safe at the ranch."

We broke up and went our separate ways. Tracy and me went back to our cabin and unloosed the cats. We let them play in the long grass behind the cabins, where they found stuff to chase. Mayhew and Eben were getting as big as bobcats and acted just as wild.

"They're such fun," said Tracy, laughing. "Thanks for getting them for us." I'd given the brace of kittens to Tracy for Christmas before we were married. "Why did Doctor Rumdab have to bring up the murder?"

"I'm surprised no one brought it up earlier. You'd think it'd be preying on people's minds. I guess the dudes are determined to have fun no matter what."

"Do you think Sheriff Fish has really caught the killer?"

"I doubt it. Drew probably just told us that to make us feel safe."

"Three murders in two years. That's bad luck for a dude ranch."

"It's bad luck for any place of business," I said. "You'd think with all the horseshoes around they'd have nothing but good luck."

We each grabbed a cat and headed around to the front of the cabins. Agnes Weatherby's DeSoto was just headed down the road. Ned was driving and Margot was behind him in an old Plymouth. They both honked and waved.

"You know those people?" asked Tracy.

"Yeah. Ned and Margot. My long lost cousins. A couple of nuts who live with Panhandle's aunt. It looks like they just picked up Miss Weatherby's borrowed car."

"I hope you're through with that gang."

"You and me both."

We went into the cabin and took a long nap, though neither of us slept.

Supper consisted of steak—from Buckaroo-raised beef—mashed potatoes and gravy, string beans, and some lousy Jell-O full of grated vegetables. There was chocolate cake for dessert. The steaks were a bit chewy, but the flavor was good. We rested our guts for a while and then headed into the grub house for the square dance. They'd cleared the tables to one side and strung colorful banners from the ceiling. Bow-legged Sheepy was up on a soap box warming up his fiddle. He played like he knew what he was doing. Hawk, the lady killer, was there to call the dance.

All the dudes were dressed to the nines—maybe even the tens—in fancy Western garb. Tracy wore a turquoise dress with a flouncy skirt and stripes of silver sequins. I wore new jeans and a red and yellow cowboy shirt with lots of pearl buttons, and a showy neckerchief. We all stomped around and got in each other's way and stepped on a few toes. But everyone was laughing and sweating and having fun.

Sheepy was practically foaming at the mouth by the time he stopped fiddling. It was late before the dance broke up. Hawk announced that we'd be going on a hayride in the morning. We caught our breath for the last time and moseyed off to our different cabins. Nobody wanted to take a shower until morning. The facilities were primitive and the water was always cold.

"That was some fun," Tracy told me, as we stepped inside our home away from home. "You dance like Fred Astaire."

"Sure. Fred Astaire with lead in his shoes. You make a good Ginger Rogers, though."

We took the cats out for a late spin and then went to bed. About midnight there was a knock at our door. I answered it in the red plaid robe Tracy had given me for the trip. It was Lilly Rumdab, and she looked worried. Her hair was sticking out all over and she wore a robe over a nightgown.

"What's up?" I asked her.

Tracy came up behind me.

"I've asked everybody else," said Lilly. "Yours is the last cabin. I can't find my husband. No one's seen him."

"Maybe he went out for a smoke," I said, "or to get a breath of air."

"Karl doesn't smoke, and he wouldn't go out at night with a murderer loose. I'm worried. I woke up and he wasn't in bed next to me. Where can he be?"

"We'll find him," I said. "Don't worry."

"I'm so sorry," said Tracy. "I'm sure your husband is fine. We'll help look for him. You look really sleepy, Lilly."

"I can hardly keep my eyes open. I don't know what's wrong with me. Thank you for offering to help find Karl."

Even without her makeup Lilly looked pretty classy under our porch light.

"Just give us a minute to get dressed," I told her. "We'll be right out. We'll find the doc."

"I'm going up to the ranch house to wake Mr. Breedlaw," said Lilly. "I hate to, but I don't know what else to do."

"Sure," I said. "We'll catch up with you."

I closed the door and we got dressed.

"Are you thinking what I'm thinking?" asked Tracy, pulling on jeans and a sweatshirt.

"The doc hasn't been murdered, Tracy. Don't even think that. Maybe he went up to the grub house to get a midnight snack. Or maybe he's having a moonlit amour with Audra or Sissy Dell, though I doubt it."

I finished dressing, stuck my thirty-eight in my pocket, and grabbed my flashlight off the nightstand. We went out into the night. The stars looked close enough to grab and there was a moon. While we were passing the other cabins, Curt poked his head out his door. He was dressed.

"Did Lilly find her husband?" he asked, in a whisper.

"No," I said. "We're going to help her find him. Lilly went up to the ranch house to rouse Breedlaw. He'll likely wake up the buckaroos. Do you have a flashlight?"

"In my car. I'll get it. I'll see if Walter wants to help search."

"Good. We'll meet you up by the grub house."

I noticed that the Rumdab's Citroen was still in the parking lot. Folks were already gathering at the chuck house. Breedlaw and Lilly were standing out front. Panhandle and Hawk and Sheepy were coming down from the bunkhouse. In a minute, Audra and Drew showed up, then Curt and Walter. That made eleven of us. We decided to break up into pairs, with Curt coming with me and Tracy. Walter had a flashlight with him and Breedlaw fetched a couple more from the chuck house. He already had one with him. That gave each couple a flashlight with one to spare.

"Maybe you should go back to your cabin," Breedlaw told Lilly.

"I can't. I'm going with you. It's my husband. Where could he be?"

"We'll find him," said Breedlaw, tugging at his mustache.

There were several trails leading from the ranch buildings. I picked one at random and Tracy and Curt started playing bloodhound. Curt had kept his flashlight and I had mine.

"I hope this is going to turn out all right," said Tracy.

"You don't think it could be Jack the Roper, do you?" Curt asked.

I stopped in my tracks. "How'd you hear about the Roper?"

"Sissy Dell was telling Mabel about him this afternoon. She didn't want to talk about it, but Mabel got it out of her. The guy's killed three people."

"Likely only two," I said. "Brice's killer wanted us to think he was the Roper, but I guess it doesn't matter. One killer's as good as another."

The trail I'd picked led into some dense forest. The trees blocked out the moonlight and we had to depend on our flashlights. We all three stumbled now and then. Both Curt and me shined our lights around at the sides of the trail. Maybe Rumdab had strayed from the path for some reason. It had rained a little in the afternoon, but the pine trees all around us had kept the rain off the ground; we couldn't find any footprints. A little wind was picking up and making us cold. We'd gone far enough that when we looked behind us we could no longer see the lights Breedlaw had left on in the grub house.

After we'd walked what I figured was close to half a mile, I thought about turning back. I didn't see why the doctor would have gone this far. Then Tracy saw something ahead of us.

"Shine your light on that big tree in front of us again," she said.

Both me and Curt aimed our lights at a tall aspen about twenty feet ahead of us. Something was dangling from one of its branches. We hurried forward. Dr. Karl Rumdab was hanging like the victim of an old West lynching. A rope was around his skinny neck, the other end thrown over a tree branch and tied off at the base of the tree.

His feet were no more than a foot off the ground. When I reached up and touched his neck it was still warm. I got out my jackknife and reached up and cut the rope. I heard Tracy gasp.

"Lordy!" said Curt, whispering. "Is he—?"

Once I had him laid out on the ground, I loosened the rope around his neck and felt for a pulse. "He's dead as a mackerel," I said. I felt of his neck again. It didn't appear to be broken. The doc's dead face was dark and swollen. The eyes bulged and the tongue stuck out. I tried to keep Tracy from getting too good a view of the dead croaker. I flashed my light around for any sign of footprints or anything else. There was nothing. "We need to get back and call the sheriff. And somebody's going to have to tell Lilly. I'm just glad she's not the one who found him."

"Should one of us stay here with the body?" asked Curt. His voice was shaking.

"That's not a good idea," I said. "The killer might still be out here somewhere. I don't think this was suicide. Let's go. I hope no animal comes along and makes a meal off of Rumdab." I turned to Tracy who was right at my shoulder. "You all right?"

"Yes," she said in a quavery voice. "This is my first dead body."

"I'm sorry I dragged you out here. I just set up a whole string of nightmares for you."

"You didn't drag me. I wanted to come. I'm OK, just a little shook. Let's go back. Poor Lilly.

That body could be yours, Axe." She shivered.

"Not a chance. I plan on sticking around for a long time. Curt? You OK?"

"I feel kind of sick," he said. He turned and threw up in some bushes.

"That's right, get it out of your system," I said. "Let's hit the trail. The sooner we're back the sooner the sheriff can get a look at this body."

We went back a lot quicker than we'd come. A few folks were inside the dining hall. Sissy Dell was there and she'd made coffee. Walter and Hawk had given up and come back from whatever trail they'd been on. Sheepy and Panhandle had given up too. That left Lilly and Breedlaw, and Audra and Drew, still out searching.

"Honk a car horn to get the others to come back," I told Hawk. "And call the sheriff. We found the doc. He's dead, with a rope around his neck."

"Hell's bells," said Hawk. "I'll make the phone call. One of you others go honk your car horn."

"I'll do it," said Walter. He looked more mournful than ever. He got out of his chair and headed out the door.

9

The honking worked. Within twenty minutes, the other searchers had returned. I wasn't looking forward to facing Lilly. She came into the grub house on Breedlaw's arm, looking pale and scared.

"Is he here?" she asked. "My husband? Is Karl all right?"

I stepped forward to talk to the new widow, but Tracy beat me. She put an arm around Lilly.

"The doctor's had an accident," Tracy told Lilly. "You need to sit down."

Breedlaw got a chair under her before her legs gave out. She started shaking and gave Tracy a pleading look full of tears.

"He's gone, Lilly. We found him. I don't think he suffered."

Lilly wailed like a coyote and beat her fists on the arms of the chair. We all came forward and mumbled a bunch of useless words.

"Maybe we need to get her back to her cabin," I said, "but she can't stay there by herself. And, for

God's sake, get her a drink."

Sissy Dell turned to Panhandle. "Get the whiskey bottle," she told him. "Bring it to her cabin." She led Lilly out the door, glancing sadly over her shoulder at the rest of us.

"What happened?" asked Breedlaw. His voice sounded a bit slurred. He'd been babysitting a bottle. "Who found the doc?"

Tracy and Curt and me gave him the story.

"We found him hanged from a tree a good half-mile from here," I said. "He was dead, but his neck wasn't broken. We didn't find any tracks or anything else. I didn't think to go through his pockets. There might be a note on him."

"Why a note?" asked Breedlaw. "This is terrible, just terrible!"

"He didn't go out in the woods in the middle of the night for no reason," I said. "He was scared of the guy who killed Holcombe. He didn't tell his wife where he was going, and he snuck out of their cabin. I think he slipped Lilly a mickey. Easy enough for a doc to do. I believe he thought he was meeting a lady."

"You think a woman did this?" asked Breedlaw. He clearly didn't believe me.

"I didn't say that. The note could have been a fake. But, yeah, a dame could have done it. Rumdab was a small guy. The killer likely slipped the noose over Rumdab's head when his back was turned, then threw the rope over a limb and leveraged him off his feet. A woman could have done it. She might have knocked him on the head before putting the rope around his neck."

"What kind of a knot was in the rope?" asked Breedlaw, getting a crafty look on his weathered face.

"I couldn't say. It wasn't a hangman's noose. Probably just a slipknot. I don't know if it was a Honda knot."

Breedlaw stared at me. "Who you been talking to, Hatchett?"

I shrugged. "It doesn't matter. I've heard about the Roper, but I think we all have by now."

"You think the same man who killed my wrangler killed Rumdab?"

"Of course. There can't be that many murderers running around."

Breedlaw ran his fingers through his silver hair. The others gathered around and asked a bunch of questions all at once. I saw something out the front window. Headlights were coming up the road. The sheriff had arrived. He and his deputy got out of the car and came inside.

"Everybody here?" Sheriff Fish asked Breedlaw.

"Yeah," said Breedlaw. "Except for the dead man's wife, and Sissy Dell. They're in the dead man's cabin."

"Who found the body?" asked Fish, looking around at all of us.

Me and Tracy and Curt all raised our hands, like school kids. "Two of you are coming with me.

I need you to show me where the body is."

"I'll go," I said. "It's a lovely night for a stroll."

"Me, too," said Tracy.

Fish looked at her and took off his hat. "This isn't something a lady should get herself involved in, ma'am."

"I helped find the body," said Tracy.

"It'd be better if you stayed here, ma'am, and helped with the widow. She'll want all the women folk around her that she can get."

Tracy glared at him but he wasn't going to budge. Curt stepped forward and said he'd come along. Mabel grabbed his arm.

"It's not safe," she told him. "I don't want you going."

"He'll be safe with us, ma'am," said the sheriff. "Me and my deputy are armed. Nothing to worry about." He turned to the others. "The rest of you folks can stay here or go back to your cabins. We'll be talking to you later. I know it's late, but that's the way it's going to be. I don't want any of you taking any walks or driving anywhere. I hate to say it, but you're all suspects."

There was a collective gasp. Fish raised his arms in the air for quiet. "None of you's got anything to worry about. I'm just doing my job."

That was that. Folks started heading for their cabins. The Buckaroo hands stayed put. I walked Tracy to our cabin, telling Fish I'd be right back.

"I wish I was going with you," Tracy told me, when we were halfway to our place.

"You wouldn't like it. They'll be all night fussing over the body. I don't know when I'll get back."

We reached our cabin and I pulled my snubnose from my pocket.

"Keep this close," I said.

"No. You keep it. You might need it."

"I'll grab my automatic from the truck. It's in the glove box."

"OK. When you come back, knock before you come in."

"Sure. Keep the door locked. I'll give you the whole story when I get back."

We kissed goodbye and I fetched my Browning from the truck and stuck it in my belt. I still had my flashlight. I joined Fish and his deputy at the grub house. Curt had grabbed a jacket from his cabin. I wished I'd done the same. It was getting cold.

The sheriff looked at the gun I had stuck in my belt.

"You must be the detective fellow," he said.

"You've been checking up on us, have you?"

"Just doing my job."

I got the feeling the sheriff said that a lot.

"Let's go look at Doc Rumdab," he told me and Curt. "I hope no coyotes have gotten to the body."

"There's no blood," I said. "That helps. We'll have to carry the stiff back with us. We need some kind of stretcher."

"I've got a blanket in the trunk of the car," said

Fish.

"That won't work." I said. "I wonder if there's a folding cot on the ranch we can borrow. That would work swell. I'll ask Breedlaw if he's still around."

I went back outside and looked around. I found Breedlaw sitting at a table in back of the grub house, pulling at his mustache. He looked like he'd rather be someplace else. He looked up when I shined my flashlight in his face.

"You got a folding cot I can borrow?" I asked him.

He stared at me.

"What do you want that for?" he asked.

"I thought I'd take a nap, what else? We need some kind of stretcher to bring out Rumdab's remains."

"Oh. We keep some cots in the barn for when folks bring their kids along. I'll go fetch one."

"Tell me where they are and I'll do it myself."

"OK. They're in the loft. We store stuff up there."

"Thanks."

I followed my flashlight beam to the old barn. There were some horses in the stalls. I hoped I wouldn't wake any of them. I climbed the rickety ladder to the hay loft, tracked down a folding cot and managed to bring it down the ladder with me without falling and breaking my neck. I carried it up to the grub house and went out back where the pallbearers were waiting.

"Let's get going," I told everyone. "I'll carry this thing until I get tired and then one of you others can spell me."

"That was a right fine idea of yours," said Fish. "That cot will make a fine stretcher. We'll walk side by side, if we can. That way we'll be able to look at the whole trail before any of us make new footprints and ruin the crime scene."

"Is the coroner on his way?" I asked.

"No," said Fish, "I couldn't get ahold of him. Didn't answer the damned phone. I think he sleeps with earplugs."

"Why not send somebody over to his house?"

"That's a right fine idea, too. Wished I'd thought of it. Not much he can do in the dark anyway."

Sheriff Fish and his deputy, who called himself Lathe, each had a big flashlight. They shined the beams on the trail in front of us. It was a dirt track, worn into the ground by a generation or more of horseshoes. It was hard-packed and not conducive to showing the prints of murderers. We went very slowly. The wind picked up and there was the smell of rain in the air. Some lazy thunder rolled through the sky. I was really wishing I'd brought my jacket. My long-sleeved cowboy shirt wasn't much for warmth. Curt had his jacket, and so did both the law enforcement boys. The temperature was still dropping.

"How far along do we have to go?" Fish asked me.

"I'd guess we aren't even halfway there yet. The trail's pretty straight and level, though. We'll get there."

"Never thought I'd be spending my vacation like this," said Curt. He sounded more excited than disappointed. He'd have something to tell the folks in Iowa about.

I wasn't exactly sure where we'd found the body, but in the end we practically stumbled over it. The doc looked small, and limp, and very much alone. His face was an ugly purple mask in the light from the flashlights.

"Why'd you cut him down?" Fish asked me. He sounded mad.

"Why do you think? I thought he might still be alive. When I touched his neck it was still warm, so I thought he might be playing possum."

"He sure ain't. Looks like the last one, poor Brice. The knot on the rope's different, though."

"Don't tell me, a Honda knot?"

"That it is."

"I guess our murderer's learning. Too bad he slipped up the first time."

"Maybe it's a different killer."

"Three different murderers in two years?" I asked. "And all on the same ranch?"

"Yeah, don't seem likely. You two fellows stay back. Me and Lathe's got work to do."

I set down the folding cot. I'd carried the damned thing under my arm the whole way, like a sap.

The sheriff and his deputy shined their lights all over the area. They found a couple of faint footprints that might have belonged to me, or anyone. Fish got out a measuring tape and Lathe pulled out a Polaroid camera from a canvas bag he had slung over his shoulder. He took a bunch of pictures, the flash bulbs practically blinding us. Lathe even got out a magnifying glass, and damned if he didn't find something. A dame's dangly earring. They searched the pockets of the corpse but didn't find anything you wouldn't ordinarily find in a man's pockets. No love note.

Curt and me stayed to one side, shifting from one foot to another. I shivered and cursed myself for not having grabbed my jacket from the cabin.

"You think a woman killed the doctor?" he asked me.

"You mean the earring? It could be a plant. Why would a lady murderer be wearing fancy earrings out in the woods?"

"If she wanted the doc to think she was trying to look her best for him. Maybe she met him earlier along on the trail and lured him up here."

"That's a thought. You like playing detective?"

"Right now I'd give up the opportunity just to get back to a fire."

"I know how you feel. Maybe they'll be done soon."

The lawmen fussed around for a while more. Then we got the cot unfolded and put the doc to bed. Even dead, he didn't weigh much.

"I guess we're ready," Fish told us. "Lathe, you and me will take the front end, and these two gentlemen can take the feet."

That's what we did. We started off down the trail. It was a long trip back, but at least the exercise warmed me up some.

When we finally got back to the ranch buildings, Fish suggested we put the body on a table in the chuck house.

"This'll make breakfast interesting," I said.

Fish told Lathe to go to the car and get on the radio and have someone go rouse up the coroner. There was nobody but us grave robbers in the grub house. Somebody had been thoughtful enough to build a fire in the big pot-bellied stove. The heat felt good. Everybody else had gone to bed. I was a little surprised no one had waited up for us, not even Breedlaw, but he was no doubt expecting a pretty full day. While Lathe was out squawking on the radio, Fish talked to me and Curt. We'd found a table cloth to cover the body, and the three of us sat at the same table — to keep the doc company I guess — and Fish told us what was going to happen.

"We'll need to question all of you," the sheriff said, "but it's too damned early in the morning. We'll let you folks rest for a while, at least until Rory, the coroner, gets up here. Why don't you two go back to your cabins? Thanks for your help, by the way. I'm going to try to get some shut-eye in my car. I figure we'll get everybody together around breakfast time."

Curt and I didn't wait for a second invitation. We headed off for bed. A light was still burning in my cabin. I remembered to knock.

"Who's there?" Tracy called through the closed door.

"The undertaker."

She opened the door. She was still dressed. Eben and Mayhew were both on the bed, stretched out to take up as much room as possible.

"You sure took your time," said Tracy. "Are you all right?"

"I'm OK. We had to carry Rumdab back with us. The coroner will be up here in a while. You should be asleep."

"So should you. Let's get in bed and pull up the quilt. Our little heater doesn't give out much heat."

We got into bed with our clothes on and pulled up the crazy quilt. Both cats woke up, yawned, and went back to sleep.

"Did you or the sheriff find any clues?" Tracy asked.

"Nothing worth putting in your diary. A couple of footprints, maybe yours. An earring."

Tracy sat up. "An earring! That's important. You think the killer is a woman?"

"I doubt it. The earring is probably a plant. Why would a dame dress up to kill somebody?"

"So she'd look good in case she got caught. Was it a clip earring, or one for pierced ears?"

"Damned if I know."

"You should have noticed. Find out from the sheriff. If it's a clip then it could belong to any of the ladies. But if it's for a pierced ear, we'll have to look at the suspect's ears. Anything else?"

"Well, the knot in the rope. A regular slipknot was used for the first killing. Rumdab's rope was tied with a Honda knot."

"So our killer is learning how to tie his knots," said Tracy.

"Don't refer to him as 'our' killer."

"No? You squeamish?"

"I just hope we're not next on his list, that's all. We should try to get some sleep."

"I can't stop thinking about Lilly."

"She'll be OK. Who knows? She may not even have liked her husband."

"I like mine."

"I'll try to keep it that way," I said. "Now close your eyes and start counting sheep."

"This is cattle country, partner."

"Sorry. Count cows then."

We actually managed to sleep a couple of hours, until dawn. I went and peeked out the window. The coroner's wagon was back, and there was a black-and-white cop's car parked behind the sheriff's jalopy. Fish was standing in the parking lot, talking to a fat officer in a blue uniform. Fish was waving his arms. So was the man in blue. They were probably arguing about some jurisdiction issue. Somebody was stepping on somebody else's toes.

"Who's out there?" Tracy asked from the bed.

"Bunch of law and order boys. We're in for it now. They're going to want to interrogate all of us."

"Will they torture us first?"

"They'd love to, but their hands are tied legally. They'll have to treat us almost like people."

"Poor Lilly. Will they grill her too?"

"Sure, or maybe boil her. She's a suspect. She might have killed her own husband."

"You think so? She was awfully upset."

"She needs to act her part, doesn't she?" I asked.

Tracy got out of bed. "Let's go talk to the cops and see what's going on."

"No. They won't tell us anything."

"They might tell me something. I'm not their natural enemy. I'm not a private investigator. I want to find out about that earring. If it was for a pierced ear, we can start checking out the women around here. The dudes and the ranch girls."

"I'm sure it was a plant."

"Come on, let's go talk to somebody. It won't kill you."

"Do you really want me to get involved in this? What if old Primus Roan wants to hire me?"

"You can always say no."

"Some people can't say no." I thought of Agnes Weatherby.

Tracy got her coat and handed me mine.

112

"Your gun's on the nightstand," she said. "You want it?"

"I'll leave it here. No point in making the gendarmes nervous."

We had to shoo the cats away from the door. They wanted part of the action.

10

Outside, it was cold and clammy and still almost dark. An invisible sun barely brightened a dull, cloudy, sky. A cop got out of the passenger's side of the cruiser and came over to us.

"You folks are confined. You'll have to return to your quarters."

"I'm a detective," I told him. I dug out one of my business cards. The cop was built like an anvil, short and solid. "I just want to look around, talk to some people. I know it's early, but there might be a cowboy or two in the barn. I won't interfere with the official investigation."

"You'll need to return to your quarters." He casually rested his ham of a hand on the butt of his holstered revolver.

"My husband is working for Primus Roan," said Tracy. "This is his ranch."

"Ma'am, you need to return to your quarters."

"Yeah?" I said. "Let me ask the sheriff. I think this is his jurisdiction. Is he in the dining hall?"

"I can't let you disturb him."

"We aren't disturbing anyone," I said "We're just going to the barn. If it'll make you feel any better you can give me a ticket for jaywalking."

We started for the barn.

"Hey!" the cop called after us. "I'll have to report this."

Tracy turned and waved at the guy. "Give your boss a big hello from me."

We kept walking and the cop left us alone.

"I'm not working for Primus Roan," I told Tracy.

"Sure you are. He just doesn't know it yet."

The morning dew settled on the shoulders of our jackets and Tracy's hair. I was wearing my fedora. There were a couple of latticed windows in the barn and we were happy to see some yellow light showing through them.

"Ranch hands get up early," said Tracy.

"You don't seem to be that much of an early bird."

"I've been corrupted by city life, and by you."

One wing of the big barn door was open and we went inside. The bandy-legged Sheepy was dabbing something from a paint pot onto a sorrel horse's hoof. The cowboy turned when he heard us crossing the straw-strewn floor.

"Howdy folks!"

"You're up early," I said.

"I always am, but I'm up even earlier this morning. Couldn't sleep. That damned killing.

What's this world coming to?"

"An end," I said, "but I hope not before breakfast. You putting glue on the horses' hooves? Aren't they slow enough already?"

"I'm just patching a split. These horses with light colored hooves, they split easier. You're right about our horses. They ain't much. Mr. Roan don't care about the dude ranch no more. All he cares about is his fancy studs. Never used to be that way. You seen the roofs on our buildings?"

"As swaybacked as some of your hay burners," I said.

"Yep. Mr. Roan don't want to spend no money on fixing them."

"Why is that?" asked Tracy. She'd found a straw to chew on.

"Well, the place ain't been the same since them killings a couple of years ago. Hurt our business some. And now here we got two new killings. Makes a man want to spit."

"Go ahead," I said. "We'll turn our heads."

Sheepy spat into a pile of straw. I think it made him feel better.

"I'm a private investigator," I told him. "Nobody's hired me to look into the murders, but I've got some professional curiosity."

"That so? You one of them detectives like on TV?"

"No, those guys are chumps. I'm the real thing. Do you have any idea who might have murdered Brice Holcombe or Karl Rumdab?"

He finished with the hoof, put his pot of goo away on a worn shelf, and came over to talk to us. "Some town folks, I figure. Maybe high school kids. The way they drive their cars is a caution, I'm telling you. I figure it was some of them that shot up our sign."

"Plugging holes in a sign is a whole lot different from strangling folks," I said.

"I reckon. But once you get started on the wrong side of the law, where does it stop?"

"Do all you Carefree Buckaroos get along?"

"You saying one of us killed Brice?" He glowered at me and spat in the straw again. "Pardon me, Ma'am," he said to Tracy.

"What's a little spit between friends?" she said. "My husband's just trying to get together a list of suspects. Clearing the names of your friends on the ranch is a good start."

"Well, we all get along fine. Nobody had nothing against Brice. He was a good wrangler and kept to himself."

"Any little romances going on at the ranch?" I asked.

"I'm too old and stove up for any of that, but when you get heifers and bulls together there's going to be some spooning. Hawk's blood is too hot, and he's always got an eye on the lady dudes. Drew's sweet on Sissy Dell, but it don't do him no good. Hawk's partial to her as well, but—ain't it funny?—with his looks and ways, she still don't give him the time of day."

"Did Holcombe have any girlfriends?" Tracy asked.

"Well, he and Audra talked over the fence more than a time or two. And Sissy Dell was partial to him. That riled Hawk. He couldn't see why she'd have cow eyes for Brice and none for him. He's stuck on himself, that Hawk is."

"Is he a real cowpoke?" Tracy asked. "I don't like his clothes."

"Yeah, he's hell for duds. He grew up around here, but then he went off to that Hollywood. Couldn't act for beans, I hear, so he come on home. The lady dudes, they can't get enough of him."

"Does Breedlaw behave himself?" I asked. "I know he's married."

"He don't look at the ladies none. He don't bother Sissy Dell or Audra none. He's in love with John Barleycorn."

"What about this batch of dudes you've got up here now? Have any of them talked bad about Rumdab that you've heard?"

"I ain't saying nothing bad about the dead. You talked to him, what did you think of him?"

"He had some rough edges, but he seemed to get along with folks OK." I said. "What about his wife, Lilly? Do you think she and her husband were getting along?"

"Near as I could tell, they didn't fight more than most married folks. You don't think she killed him, do you?"

"No, just trying to cover all the bases. Thanks for talking to us."

"Who has pierced ears around here?" asked Tracy.

"I don't pay no attention. You talking about the earring they found? Breedlaw told me about it. Was it for a pierced ear?"

"I haven't heard," said Tracy. "The sheriff or the cops talk to you yet?"

"No. I went to bed after talking to Mr. Breedlaw. I reckon they'll be talking to us this morning. Is that police car still here?"

"It was when we came down to the barn," I said. "Listen, we'll be seeing you later. Thanks for chewing the fat with us."

"Yeah," he looked at Tracy. "Ma'am, you sure can ride a horse."

"Thanks," she said, and colored up like a school girl.

We left the barn and walked over to the chuck house. The cop car was gone and so was the coroner's wagon.

"I wonder if they've got the coffee pot on," I said to Tracy. "I could use a cup."

We tried the front door and it was unlocked. The sheriff and his deputy were inside, along with Panhandle and Sissy Dell. Panhandle was yawning and his eyes were about half closed. Breedlaw came out of the kitchen with a tin cup of coffee in one hand.

"Do you mind if a couple of us dudes have

some coffee?" I asked.

"Help yourselves. It's in the kitchen."

I looked at the sheriff. "You mind our being in here?"

"No," said Fish. "We're about done. I figure you folks can have your breakfast, same as usual. You two and the other dudes. Then I'm going to have to talk to all of you."

"That figures," I said.

"Do you have a lot of murders in this part of the state?" asked Tracy.

Fish bristled. "Outside of this ranch, no. I wish they'd shut down the dude ranch. I wish Mr. Roan would sell the whole place, lock, stock, and barrel."

"It's a nice place," said Tracy.

"Well, ma'am, it ought to be. It looks to be a good place. But four murders in two years makes it look like New York City. This ranch is a bigger spot of trouble than the whole rest of the county."

"Did they ever catch who did the first two murders?" Tracy asked.

"We have our ideas, ma'am, but nobody's gone to jail for it. Likely the Roper's dead. You heard of him?"

"Hasn't everyone?" I said.

"Who do you think it was?" asked Tracy.

"I'm sorry to say it, but I'm not free to tell you that. No offence meant."

"None taken," said Tracy. "I wanted to ask you about the earring that you found near Dr. Rumdab's body. Was it for a pierced ear?"

"Did you lose an earring?" He seemed suddenly interested.

"No. I wouldn't wear earrings up here. I'm not that much of a dude. I was just interested. What's it look like?"

"That information is part of our investigation, ma'am. Sorry."

"I got a glimpse of it, Tracy," I said. "It was a silver dangly thing, shaped like a cowboy boot."

"How cute. Did you notice how it attached to the ear?"

"It was for a pierced ear," I lied. I wanted to see how Fish would respond.

"Since your husband already knows. ma'am, I guess I can tell you. It was for a pierced ear. I don't suppose you've seen any of the dudes wearing those kind of earrings, have you?"

"Dangly ones?" asked Tracy. "Betsy was wearing some yesterday. But since her hair was down for once, I didn't really get a good look at them."

"Thanks for the information, ma'am."

"I'm not saying Betsy is a murderer," said Tracy, hastily. "She sure has an eye for the men, though."

"You think she might have met with the doc out in the woods?" asked the sheriff.

"Maybe. It's more likely she lost an earring and the murderer found it and left it near the body, to try to frame Betsy," said Tracy.

"Why would the killer want to do that?"

"Just to put suspicion on someone else. That's all I mean."

"Listen, folks," said Fish, "since you're already here, and the other dudes aren't up yet, why don't we go ahead and question you. It'll mean less work for me and Lathe after breakfast."

"Sounds swell to me," I said. "Let me go get some coffee."

"Two cups?" asked Sissy Dell. "I'll get them for you. Cream and sugar?"

"Black for me and a little sugar for my wife. Thanks."

She hopped off her stool and went to fetch our coffee. I noticed what a really pretty girl she was. Fluffy palomino hair, bright blue eyes, a scattering of freckles on a creamy complexion, and delicate features. She had a nice walk, too. I could see why Hawk and Drew might be smitten with her.

Fish turned to Breedlaw. "Is there a private place where me and Lathe can talk to these folks?"

"There's the pantry," said Breedlaw. "There's a table in there, and we can carry in some chairs."

Sissy Dell brought out two tin cups of coffee and handed them to me and Tracy. I picked up a bar stool and Tracy took another. The sheriff and his deputy each grabbed a stool as well. Breedlaw took us into the kitchen and to a large pantry off to one side. Breedlaw turned on a light for us and closed the door on his way out.

"This will work fine," said Fish. "Lathe, you're taking notes."

Lathe dragged a pen and pad of paper out of a shirt pocket and we all sat down.

"All right," said the sheriff, "let's get started. First of all, what time did you folks go to bed last night?"

"I don't remember the time," I said. "It was a while after the square dance, whenever that broke up. Tracy and I sat outside our cabin for an hour or so, drinking champagne. It's our honeymoon."

"Congratulations to the both of you," said Fish. "You didn't get drunk or anything, did you?"

Tracy laughed. "No, sir. We stayed pretty sober."

"What'd you do after you drank your wine?"

"Went to bed," I said.

"You didn't take a little stroll or anything first?"

"No stroll," said Tracy.

"Did either of you get up during the night?"

"No," I said. "We slept until Lilly Rumdab woke us up by knocking on our cabin door."

"Hear any noises during the night? Like somebody's cabin door opening? Footsteps? Arguments?"

"We didn't hear a sound until Lilly woke us up," said Tracy. "We were pretty tired, and we'd had two bottles of champagne. Small bottles."

"I know you've only been here for a couple of days, but have you noticed anybody not getting along with the others? Was Doc Rumdab easy to get along with?"

"He wasn't all that friendly," said Tracy. "I

don't know if anybody really got along with him. He was OK, just a little cranky. I never heard anyone say much against him."

"Not much? But a little? Somebody complained to you about him?"

"Just my husband, Axe. He didn't care much for the doctor, but he didn't think he was all that bad either."

Thanks Tracy, I thought.

"I see," said Fish. "Did either of you notice the doc and one of the lady dudes, or one of the ranch girls, getting friendly? You know, flirting and such? Did you see the doc paired off with anyone other than his wife?"

"Maybe Betsy," I said, "but she likes men. She likes to flirt. I don't think she means anything by it. Her husband, Walter, doesn't seem to mind."

"Has anybody said anything in your hearing about Brice Holcombe? I mean, I know he was killed the night you two arrived."

"He was likely dead before me and my wife showed up," I said.

"Right. Have you heard any of the buckaroos talking about him?"

"Just how good a guy he was," Tracy said, "and how sorry they are he got killed."

"That's all I've heard," I said. "He was a popular guy." Then I switched directions. "Is there any truth to the rumor that you've arrested someone for the murder of Holcombe?" I asked.

"No, sir. If that's what you've heard then

you've heard wrong. We got some suspects, but we haven't made any arrests. Folks, I'm about out of questions. I don't have to tell you not to leave the ranch. If you come across any information that might help us in the investigation—of both Brice and the doc's murders—make sure you pass it on to Mr. Breedlaw and he'll get ahold of me. You might as well go back to your cabin. I guess you know breakfast's going to be at seven, like usual. Are you looking forward to the hayride?" He tried to smile.

"Sure," I said, "we'll be carrying shotguns."

11

"That wasn't so bad," Tracy told me while we were walking back to our place.

"I've been through a lot worse. They must not think much of us as suspects."

"It's because you're a detective."

"It's because they don't think much of us as suspects."

"Who do you think they suspect?"

"My money would be on Walter. Betsy's a flirt, and Rumdab obviously liked attractive young women. Maybe Betsy arranged to meet the doc out in the woods and Walter found out about it. He made Betsy stay put and went out to meet the doc himself. He left Betsy's earring there to put a scare into her, make her look like a suspect. She knows Walter killed Rumdab, but she doesn't dare say a word because Walter will put the blame on her. Something like that."

"You believe that?"

"No, but I think the sheriff might."

"What about Brice Holcombe?" Tracy asked. "Why would Walter want to kill him?"

"He wouldn't. He didn't even know the guy, more than likely. I hate to say it, but there might be two murderers, plus the Roper."

"Two's always more fun."

"I'm just glad I'm not really working on this case. It'd drive me crazy. And I'd rather have you drive me crazy."

"We've got an hour before breakfast."

The sun rose higher and burned off some of the clouds, but there were still plenty of clouds left, and some thunder rolled in the distance. I thought maybe our hayride would get rained out. I doubted if anyone cared.

At a little before seven, we fed and watered the cats and left them mewing while we went to breakfast. Either folks were pretty hungry, or they were curious about Rumdab's death, because everybody showed up, even Lilly, which surprised me. Her face was puffy with crying, and she hadn't bothered to cover the damage with makeup. She sat with us and accepted our clumsy attempts at sympathy. Of course none of us talked about the murder in front of her. I think a lot of us were relieved to not talk about it.

"She's packing up to move to a motel in Quail Eye," Curt confided to us.

"We're going too," said Mabel. "We've got the room next to hers."

"You folks are leaving the dude ranch?" I

asked.

Curt shrugged. "We don't want Lilly to be alone. And, really, this isn't turning out to be much of a vacation."

"We'd like to go home," said Mabel, "but the sheriff won't let us."

"We're safe in the daytime," said Tracy. She was actually smiling. "I'm looking forward to the hayride."

"It's going to rain," said Walter. "There might not be a hayride."

Breedlaw came over and laid his hand on my shoulder. He was a lot taller than me, and since I was sitting down, he towered over me. I looked up at his face. It was serious and fatherly. I wondered what the hell he wanted.

"Can I have a word with you in private?" he said.

"Sure."

The two of us went off to the pantry. The sheriff and his deputy, their plates piled high with food, watched us leave the room. Once we were in the pantry, surrounded by shelves of canned goods and sacks of flour and sugar, Breedlaw closed the door.

"Mr. Roan would like a word with you," said Breedlaw. "Don't worry, you won't miss the hayride. We're putting it off to see if the weather clears."

"What's Primus Roan want with me?"

"You can't guess? You're a detective. He wants

to hire you to find out who murdered Brice and Dr. Rumdab."

"I'm on vacation. I'm on my honeymoon."

"Consider the circumstances. Our plans are pretty well falling apart. The dudes aren't much in the mood for enjoying hayrides, singing cowboy songs, and riding horseback. We're thinking of giving them part of their money back and sending them home as soon as the sheriff says they can go."

"I'll need to talk to my wife about this. She's my partner. She might want to talk to Roan with me."

"I don't see why that wouldn't be all right. Once you've finished eating, I'll take you on up to the big house."

"You make it sound like a prison."

"No, sir, it's a fine place. Mr. Roan ain't a bad fellow, but he's used to being in charge. That's how it's been his whole life."

"I'm ready when you are. Let me talk to Tracy."

We went back to the dining hall. I bent over Tracy and whispered in her ear: "Primus Roan wants to talk to us about the murders. He might want to hire us."

"Us?" She didn't whisper.

"Well, I thought you might want to work on another case with me. You've always wanted to."

"You mean you think if you let me in on it I might be more willing to let you ruin our honeymoon."

"Don't put it like that, and keep your screechy

voice down, will you? We're not exactly alone here."

The others were staring at us. I smiled at them unconvincingly.

"Do I get to carry one of your guns?" Tracy asked me, in a stage whisper.

"Sure. You can wear both of them."

"OK, I'm in."

We dug into our grub, and Tracy had an extra helping of pancakes.

"I'll need my energy," she said. "to chase the killer."

She got up from the table and we both left the grub house with Breedlaw.

"We'll take the truck," Breedlaw told us.

The three of us climbed into the cab of an old green Ford pickup in back of the barn. He drove us down a shortcut that consisted of twin ruts across a meadow and through some stands of trees. The log house looked just as imposing as it had the first time I'd seen it, but against a background of rain clouds it appeared less hospitable.

We all got out of the truck and went up some flagstone steps and across a broad porch. There was a big pine door with a bronze knocker shaped like a cow skull. Breedlaw hammered at the knocker. In no more than a minute the door swung inward and revealed a pudgy, middle-aged woman wearing a dark dress, a white apron, and a silly maid's cap.

"Mr. Breedlaw," she said, smiling. "We've been

expecting you. Do come in. Is this the detective?"

"And his partner," said Tracy.

We were shown into a big, high-ceilinged, entry hall. It was paneled in knotty pine, and a few deer heads sneered down on us from the walls. A wide, open, doorway gave us a view of a living room with a rock fireplace that was a little smaller than a train tunnel. A big pile of pine logs was burning in it. A buffalo head was mounted above it. On the walls on each side were big oil paintings depicting cowboys doing cowboy stuff: branding cattle, roping mustangs, sitting by an open fire with plates of beans in their laps. A gigantic hooked rug covered a fair portion of the pine floor. There was a wheelchair in front of the fire. It's occupant wheeled to face us as we entered the room.

At first I only had eyes for the chair. It was impressive — massive, with wooden-spoked wheels like a chuck wagon, tooled leather upholstery, and arms that ended in silver horse heads. The guy driving it was less impressive. For some reason I'd expected Roan to be a big guy. He wasn't, and never had been. In the big chair, the shriveled old white-haired cowboy looked no bigger than a ventriloquist's dummy.

He was dressed up in fancy boots, whipcord pants with a knife-edge crease, a gaudy rodeo shirt and a bolo tie featuring an agate the size of a Clydesdale's hoof. The little buckaroo sported a white handlebar mustache and his face was as wrinkled and bronzed as tanned alligator hide. I kind of liked him. He wheeled forward a few feet and nodded at us.

"Thank you, Mr. Breedlaw, for bringing me this detective, and his — girl Friday?"

"My wife and partner, Tracy," I said. I stepped forward and shook hands with the old fellow. He clearly made an effort to put a lot of manliness into the gesture, but he was too feeble to manage it. It was like shaking hands with a brook trout.

"My pleasure," said Roan, to Tracy. "You're a charming young woman. And your husband is a famous detective?"

"Not so famous," I said. "I try to keep a low profile. What can we do for you, Mr. Roan?"

He waved an impatient hand. "Call me Prime. My brother's name was Roundwell. Prime and Round, both steaks." He laughed in a cackling way. "Welcome to the Twin Roan's Ranch."

"I thought we were on the Carefree Buckaroo Ranch," I said.

He waved his hand again. "That is the name of the dude ranch, a mere fragment of the real ranch. My brother and I inherited a good deal of land and cattle, but we were interested in horses. Of course, we started out breeding roans — the name, you know. However, it wasn't until we'd captured and broken a bay mustang stallion that we found the stud we needed. Magnificent horse! His name was Sparkle, and he sired many a fine riding horse, and more than a few racehorses. He was the foundation of our successful horse ranch. Of course he's been dead these many years, as has Round, but his descendants still graze and propagate on Twin Roans Ranch."

The guy was as well-spoken as a Limey blue blood. I wondered where he'd been sent off to school.

"Forgive my lack of manners," the old man continued. "Can I offer you some refreshment? Coffee? Iced tea?"

"Nothing for me, thanks," I said.

"I'm fine," said Tracy.

"Well! Sit down, please. Breedlaw, you may return to the dude ranch. I'll have Sadie drive these people down when we're finished."

Breedlaw bobbed his head and left. Me and Tracy found big wing chairs, upholstered in spotted cowhide, near the fire. Roan swung his wheelchair around and parked it in front of us.

"About these murders," I started. I wanted to get right to the point.

"Excuse me," said Prime, "there has been only one murder."

"How do you figure?" I asked.

"I'm afraid Brice Holcombe took his own life. He hanged himself."

"Are you serious? I understood he was attacked and strangled."

"That possibility existed. The sheriff of course had to investigate. Sheriff Fish has been a friend of mine for years. I was friends with his older brother. Let me tell you a thing or two about Brice. Fine man, fine wrangler. He wasn't yet forty years old, but he'd been thrown by a bronc more than once. He developed arthritis. I have the same affliction, as do many folks my age. However, Brice's people were prone to a defect of the joints, as I understand it. His own father was a helpless cripple before he reached fifty. Brice could not abide the idea of ending up like his father. He was an outdoorsman and a spectacular horseman. In the last year or so, his arthritis grew quite bad. His days as a wrangler were almost over. He took some sort of pain medicine for his condition. In the end, I think it made him a bit addled. And, so, the other night, he took his horse, Skylark, and a rope, out into the woods. He slung the rope over a tree limb, tied it off to the tree trunk, placed a noose around his neck, mounted his horse, and applied the spurs. Of course, because of the actions of a killer now called Jack the Roper — you've heard of him? — Brice's death was at first considered a murder."

"Are you sure about all this?" I asked. "What about the knot in the rope? It wasn't the kind cowboys use."

"Not the kind of knot used for wrangling, but an appropriate one for hanging himself. A note was eventually found among Brice's affects, in the bunkhouse. It was found by Sheepy. You've met Sheepy?"

"We talked to him this morning," said Tracy. "He didn't say anything about your wrangler's death being a suicide."

"He was following my instructions. I wanted this whole matter of Brice's death cleared up by the sheriff and the coroner before I allowed any announcement to the dudes concerning his tragic end. If Dr. Rumdab hadn't been murdered last night, Brice's suicide would have been acknowledged to the dudes this morning."

"You mean that's changed?" asked Tracy.

"Yes. Look at the situation. We have two apparent murders. We then announce that the first murder was actually a suicide. What do we say next, that Dr. Rumdab took his own life?"

"Did he?" I asked.

"Sheriff Fish and the coroner say otherwise. We haven't yet decided what to tell the dudes. We want you people to trust and believe us. Would any of you now believe that Brice killed himself?"

"I see what you mean," I said, "but I think that's what you better do."

"You're likely right. Anyway, we have now an actual murder on our hands. It wasn't committed by Jack the Roper. He's dead."

"Does the sheriff know that?" asked Tracy.

"Yes, ma'am, he does, but he's keeping it to himself at my request. Out of respect for the Roper's widow, a fine woman."

"Was the Roper really a guy named Ezra Juniper?" I asked.

Prime raised his white eyebrows. "Yes. Have you been talking to my nephew, William? Perhaps you know him as Panhandle."

"I knew him at first as Billy," I said.

"Ah, yes." Prime licked his lips, looked at a fancy watch on his thin wrist. "If you'll excuse me, it's time for my medicine." He rang a little bell on a table by his elbow. In a half a minute, Sadie came into the room.

"Yes, sir?"

"It's time for my medicine."

I watched Sadie go over to a rustic sideboard with decanters on it and a pitcher of what I guessed was water. She poured some water into a tumbler, stirred in a teaspoon of sugar, and topped it off with what looked like whiskey. She carried the mixture over to Prime.

"Thank you, Sadie," said Prime. "In a few minutes I'll be wanting you to drive these fine folks back to the dude ranch. Have the car ready."

"Yes, sir." She curtsied and left the room.

Prime winked at me and Tracy. "Forgive an old man for his vices. There's nothing like a cold toddy to warm the bones. I'm afraid I had a bad night. The murder, you know." He took a long drink, his gullet bobbing up and down like a bucking bronco. "Where was I? Oh, yes, Dr. Rumdab. He was struck on the back of the head before being hanged. It was definitely murder. And the killer had apparently heard of Jack the Roper, knew that Brice had died by being strangled with a rope, and chose to imitate the Roper's methods."

"You said that you knew for a fact that Juniper was the Roper," I said. "How do you know that?"

"Ezra died of a stroke. On his deathbed he scribbled a note with his left hand. He confessed to his wife that he was the Roper. His widow passed the confession on to me."

"So we're definitely dealing with a new killer."

"Yes, and I want you find out who it is."

"Tell me about what the sheriff told you about Rumdab's murder. Any clues?"

"The doctor was no doubt lured into the woods by his assailant. He was struck on the head by a rock found at the scene. The only footprints found turned out to be Rumdab's. A lady's earring was found nearby. A noose was placed around the doctor's neck and he was strung up on a tree branch. A cigarette end, complete with pink lipstick, was found on the trail. A lady's handkerchief, heavily scented with perfume, was found in the doctor's pocket. A perfume called Misty Passion. It's the same brand Sheriff Fish's wife uses. That is all I have to tell you."

"Betsy, one of our fellow dudes," said Tracy, "wears pink lipstick. She also wears a lot of perfume."

"I think Betsy was set up for the murder," I said. "The cigarette, the earring, the pink lipstick. I think they were all plants."

"The sheriff agrees with you," said Prime.

"Did they ever find a note written to Rumdab, asking for a midnight assignation?" I asked.

"No. I have given you all the clues."

"Swell," I said, but I didn't really mean it.

"I want you to find the killer," said Prime. "I will pay whatever your usual fee is, and a generous bonus if you act quickly. You will of course be reimbursed for the money you paid for the dude ranch experience. All the remaining dudes will be refunded their money."

"Could I have you put all this in writing?" I asked.

"My word should be enough, but, yes, you can have it in writing."

He rang for Sadie and he asked her for pen and paper. When she brought them, he set about writing a contract, and a pretty good one. His arthritic hands made it tough for him. Tracy and I both signed the paper.

"I think we're finished," I said. "Do Tracy and I keep pretending we're dudes, or do we work on this out in the open?"

"I leave that decision up to you. Spend as much time with your fellow dudes—and the ranch hands—as possible. How else will you find out who committed the murder?"

"What if it was one of your own employees?" Tracy asked.

"Then I want them brought to justice."

Tracy and I stood up.

"You have a beautiful home," Tracy told Prime.

"Thank you, young lady. You grace it with your presence." He rang his bell again. Sadie appeared. "Drive our friends back to the dude ranch."

"Yes, sir."

12

Sadie led us outside to a foreign-built station wagon about the size of a hearse. I gathered this boat was necessary to store Prime's wheelchair when he was traveling. I hoped Sadie didn't have to load that cannon carriage by herself. Tracy and I got into the back seat and Sadie drove us down to the grub house. I noticed the Rumdab's and Halsey's flivvers were no longer in the parking lot.

"Thanks for the lift," I told Sadie. I almost tipped her.

"Yes, sir," she said, and left.

"Half the dudes are gone," said Tracy.

"Yeah, but it looks like the sun's coming out. We'll have our hayride after all."

"You seem awfully cheerful."

"Why not? I've got only one murder to solve instead of two. Trying to make a connection between Brice and the doc was giving me fits."

We went inside. Sissy Dell and Panhandle were still cleaning up the mess from breakfast.

"Where's the rest of the gang?" I asked.

Panhandle was wiping down tables. He had a cheap-smelling cigar in his mouth. "The other dudes? They're in their cabins, sulking. We told them the hayride might be off."

"The sun's shining," I said.

"Right. So I figure Sheepy will bring the hay wagon over. What fun. Did Uncle Prime spill the beans?"

"Don't talk about that, Panhandle," warned Sissy Dell. She had her ever-present smile on her face, but it looked worn out.

"It's OK," said Panhandle. "Axe here is working for the ranch now."

"Why didn't you tell me about Brice?" I asked Panhandle.

He shrugged. "That was Uncle Prime's orders. So, what did you think of the old man?"

"I think he needs a V8 to power that chair of his. He seemed all right. Where'd he get the snooty education?"

"Someplace in England. He's a real cowboy, though. So, have you figured out who knocked off the little doctor?"

"No, I need a couple of more minutes. Maybe it was you."

"I ain't a killer."

"You swipe old lady's bunnies, steal cars, and likely cheat at horseshoes. Why wouldn't you be a killer?"

"I'm telling you, I'm innocent. I didn't do any

of that. Just borrowed Auntie's car, that's all. I swear."

Tracy was talking to Sissy Dell. I went over and eavesdropped.

"Dr. Rumdab could be kind of abrasive," Tracy was saying. "He might have rubbed a few folks the wrong way. Who do you think killed him?"

Sissy Dell got a frightened look in her blue eyes. "I'm sure I don't know. Maybe it was a bear."

"A bear with a lasso," I said. "Come on, you've got to have some ideas."

"I really don't. It could have been anyone."

"Hawk?" I asked, just to stir the pot.

"No, of course not."

"Audra?" asked Tracy.

"No! None of the buckaroos would have done it."

"You saying it was one of us dudes?" I asked.

"No," said Sissy Dell. "I'm sure it wasn't. A stranger. I'll bet it was a stranger."

"Not likely," I said. "You think the doc might have had a yen for one of the ladies?"

"Why would he? He had such a pretty, young, wife."

"That wouldn't stop him," I said. "Were any of the husbands jealous of him?"

"Not that I noticed. I've got to get back to work. Excuse me." She grabbed a stack of dirty dishes and disappeared into the kitchen.

Tracy buttonholed Panhandle.

"Who's your favorite suspect?" she asked him.

"Your husband."

"Naw, he's on vacation. He only kills folks when he's working."

"He's working now. Maybe he bumped off the croaker to drum up business."

"Cute," said Tracy. "You're a funny guy. You should be on the stage, or maybe on a gallows. What'd you have against the doc?"

"I didn't like the way he made eyes at you," said Panhandle.

"Cut it out, Panhandle," I said. "You always seem to be around when nobody wants you. You must have overheard some interesting conversations."

He'd finished wiping tables and was leaning on a broom. "I noticed Betsy was making eyes at the doctor, and he didn't exactly cut her dead. I noticed the doc heckling Walter about his inventions. I seen him laughing at Mabel. The doc didn't like nobody except Betsy and your wife."

"You think Walter lured Rumdab into the woods and strung him up?" I asked.

Panhandle shrugged. "You got a better idea?"

"Sure. Curt killed him. He was wanting to make time with Betsy but she only had eyes for Rumdab. Or Lilly knocked off her husband because she'd finally had enough of his playing around. Or Audra killed the doc because she was carrying his baby and didn't want the kid to have such a sourpuss for a dad. Maybe you'll like this one. Sheepy killed Rumdab because he caught the doc feeding chewing gum to the horses. What do you think?"

"I think you're full of crap. I hope you get seasick on the hayride."

He took his broom and headed for the kitchen.

"We got nothing," Tracy told me.

"The day is young. Wait until the hayride. We'll pick up a clue or two."

"Or at least some ticks. Where's that hay wagon anyway?"

She'd scarcely spoken when we heard the jingling of harness out front.

"I think it's here," I said.

"It could be Santa."

We went out into the parking lot. The big hay wagon had seen better days and had a dry and weathered look like it was made of driftwood. It was being pulled by a brace of brown horses twice normal size. I wondered if the wagon was carrying so much hay just for the horse's lunch. Sheepy was sitting on the box, the reins in his hands, and Audra was riding shotgun, literally. She held an old double-barreled twelve gauge between her knees. I guess the buckaroos wanted us dudes to feel safe. Audra climbed down off her high chair and ran to fetch Betsy and Walter.

"Howdy folks!" Sheepy greeted us. He practically shouted with pretend joy.

"How do we get into this thing?" Tracy asked. "Does it have an elevator?"

"We got a ladder," said Sheepy. "Hang on a

minute and Audra will show you."

The curvy Audra returned with our fellow dudes in tow. Walter and Betsy looked as festive as a funeral. They were both dressed in dark cowboy clothes and their smiles weren't on their faces.

"Hi," said Betsy. She batted her eyelashes at me in a dismal sort of way.

"Let's get this over with," said Walter.

Audra went around to the back of the wagon and reached up on her tippy toes and unfastened the tailgate. She pulled a short ladder out of the hay and invited us to climb on up.

"Watch your step, folks," she said. "Don't want anybody getting hurt."

"How could anybody get hurt on a dude ranch?" asked Walter, sourly.

"Listen," said Audra, her smile fading a little. "We've got a surprise for you. We're going to stop along the way and do some trout fishing. What do you think of that?"

"I could have stayed home and gone fishing," Walter complained. "Are you making us catch our own lunch now?"

"No," said Audra, "we've got a fine lunch packed for you. But it'd be a great thing if we could add a few trout to the menu. Aren't any of you excited?"

"I am," said Tracy. I figured she was just being nice.

"I wouldn't mind outsmarting a few trout," I said.

"Outsmart?" asked Walter. "Fish are about as smart as the worms you use for bait."

"Not so," said Audra. "Trout are clever. You've got to use see-through fish line so they won't see it, and you got to bait your hook just right. We use cheese."

"Cheese for fish?" asked Betsy. "What kind of cheese?"

"Velveeta. It works best."

"How do you keep it on the hook?" asked Walter.

"Well," said Audra, "you got to cover the whole hook with the cheese, and then you dip it in the water to chill it. It stays on the hook better that way. Still, you got to be careful when you cast or that old Velveeta will end up in the bushes."

"I haven't seen any ponds or lakes around here," said Walter.

"We'll be fishing in the stream."

"What the hell?" asked Walter. "How can you tell when you've got a bite? The bobber will be bobbing all the time in a stream."

"We don't use bobbers," said Audra. "You'll be fishing tight line. You just slip your thumb or finger under the line near the reel and when a trout starts nibbling you'll feel the line jerk. It takes some practice, but you'll get the knack. Folks, let's get going."

We scaled the ladder and found spots to sit in a whole lot of hay. Audra slid the ladder back up and fastened up the tailgate. She climbed onto the box, and Sheepy whipped up the horses. They took off like a couple of mud turtles. There were picnic baskets in the hay with us. Lunch. We headed up behind the barn, the wagon creaking the whole time, and took the road that led past Primus Roan's log castle.

"You working to solve the murders?" Walter asked me.

"That's right. Me and Tracy."

"How exciting!" said Betsy, her voice like a dirge.

"What's for lunch, I wonder?" asked Tracy. She started poking at the picnic baskets.

"You hungry already?" I asked.

"A girl detective's got to keep her strength up."

The wagon rolled up the road, Sheepy keeping up a conversation with the horses, and we went past the mansion.

"Did you meet the guy that owns that place?" Walter asked me. I guessed somebody had let the secret out.

"Yep," I said. "Howdy Doody with money. He's not a bad old geezer."

"Owns this whole ranch?" asked Walter.

"Half the county, I guess. Raises horses. The dude ranch is just a sideline."

"Does he have any idea who killed Rumdab and that wrangler?" Walter asked.

"Never mind the wrangler," I said. "That's all solved. Rumdab was the only person who was murdered."

"That so?"

"Ask Sheepy and Audra."

I was interested in seeing what they'd say. Walter was sitting near the back of the wagon. He sailor-walked his way to the front, stepping carefully through the hay. When he got to the seat, he hung on to its back and talked to the pair of buckaroos.

"Hey," I heard him say, "the detective here says your wrangler wasn't murdered. Is that so?"

Sheepy jumped like he'd been struck with his own horse whip. "I guess the cat's out of the bag. Brice likely killed himself, poor fellow."

"It wasn't the Roper?" asked Walter.

"Forget about the Roper. That's all in the past. Brice was all busted up, and stove up, and in a mort of pain. Looks like he strung himself up."

"Why didn't you tell us?" complained Walter.

"Took a while to sort things out. We was fixin' to tell you," said Sheepy.

"So the doctor's the only one who was murdered."

"Looks like."

"I think Hawk did it," said Walter.

"Why Hawk?" asked Sheepy, turning to give Walter a pop-eyed stare. "You're barking up the wrong tree, son."

"No, I'm not. Hawk was making passes at Betsy. She told him to go shove it. Then Rumdab started flirting with my wife. I told him to stop it, and he did. But I think Hawk was jealous. Hawk might have believed Betsy would change her mind about him if the doctor was out of the way."

"You're fishing in a dry creek," said Sheepy. "What you're saying don't make no sense."

Betsy made her clumsy way to the front of the wagon. "You're just jealous," she told Walter. "I don't care about Hawk. He's all show. If he'd killed the doctor, why would he leave my earring by the body to make it look like I did it?"

"Don't talk about that," Walter warned her, looking over at me and Tracy.

"That earring was yours, Betsy?" asked Tracy.

"Yes. I bought those earrings for the trip. And then I lost one of them, yesterday. I didn't kill the doctor, and I didn't meet him out in the woods. I think the sheriff thinks I did. Meet him in the woods, I mean."

"The earring was a plant," I said. "Don't worry, they can't use it against you. The sheriff knows you're not the killer. Do you think if someone wrote a love note to Rumdab, and signed your name to it, he'd have gone out in the woods to meet you?"

"No. He was scared to death of the Roper. I don't see how anyone could have gotten him to go out after dark."

"Maybe he found out about Brice's death being a suicide before the rest of us did. That would have taken his fear away," I said.

"Who would have written the note?" Tracy asked me.

"It wasn't me," said Walter, bridling a bit. "I didn't want the doc dead. I wasn't jealous of him, if that's what you're thinking. Betsy flirts with all the guys. I don't know why, but I've gotten used to it. I know she wouldn't fall for a little runt like Rumdab. She likes them tall and broad-shouldered, like Hawk." He sneered a little and gave Betsy the cold fish eye.

"OK," said Tracy. "We've got to figure this out. Who around here hated the doctor enough to want him dead? Who hated him enough to kill him?"

"Maybe someone who was interested in his wife," I said. "Maybe they wanted the doctor out of the way."

"Curt was sweet on her," said Betsy. "He was all the time looking at her."

"Hell, this is getting us nowhere," I said. "Let's try something else. Who would hate Betsy enough to try to frame her for a murder? Anybody's murder."

"Hey!" said Walter. "That's my wife you're talking about."

"I know, but you said yourself that your wife likes to make eyes at every man who comes along. Maybe somebody got jealous."

"Then why not kill Betsy?" asked Tracy.

"You shut up!" said Walter.

That riled me. "Don't you go telling my wife to shut up. Maybe the killer was jealous of Betsy but couldn't figure out a way to get her off by herself so he could kill her. So, he killed Rumdab instead and tried to pin the murder on Betsy."

"Or," said Tracy, "maybe Lilly was jealous of Betsy and hated Dr. Rumdab because she thought he was going to run off with her. Betsy, I mean. So she killed two birds with one stone. She murdered her husband and made it look like Betsy did it."

I kind of liked that. Our conversation was interrupted by a desperate Audra.

"Hey, everybody!" she shouted. "Do you all know the Sierra Sue song? Let's all sing it!"

We just stared at her.

"Well, how about the Redheaded Stranger? I'll start off and you all join in."

13

Audra started warbling at the top of her lungs and after a while we grudgingly joined in, but you could tell we were still thinking of murder.

We sang a couple more songs, but they weren't bloody enough for us. Sheepy pulled the wagon into a meadow with a stream running through it.

"Folks," he said, "it looks like we might get rain after all. Let's stop here for lunch to make sure we can get back to the ranch before we have a belly buster."

"A belly buster?" asked Betsy. "What exactly are we having for lunch?"

"I mean a big rainstorm," explained Sheepy.

Audra got down from the wagon seat and came around to open the tailgate and pull down the ladder. We unloaded the picnic baskets, which were full of fried chicken and fixin's, and spread blankets on the grass and ate. We had our lunch next to a broad and meandering stream with willow growing next to it. I liked the sound of the water as it snaked its way over and around rocks. We kept a weather eye out for the coming rain and kept talking murder. Sheepy and Audra tried to stop us, but who listens to buckaroos?

"Damn it all!" I finally said. "It looks like every one of us had motive and opportunity. I need a clue if I'm going to solve this case. Something to hang a hat on. What the sheriff and his boy found doesn't help me any."

"That's all we've got," said Tracy.

Sheepy fetched the fishing tackle—fiberglass rods equipped with Zebco reels, and nets and creels for all of us. Tracy and me had done plenty of trout fishing, but Audra had to show Walter and Betsy how to bait the hooks.

"These hooks are too damned small," complained Walter. "What are we fishing for, minnows?"

"No," said Audra, "little brook trout. They're small, but they're tasty. You roll them in corn meal and fry them in a skillet. We leave the heads on."

"Ugh," said Betsy. "I don't like my meals staring back at me."

"Sissy Dell will take the heads off yours, Betsy."

We arranged ourselves along the stream bank. Tracy and me took the middle. Sheepy and Audra picked a spot upstream about forty feet. Walter and Betsy took a spot downstream. Audra warned us all to keep quiet or we'd scare the fish, but Walter kept griping about the fishing poles. He didn't like the enclosed reels, or the thin fish line, or the light poles, or much of anything. The guy was in a sour mood.

We hadn't had our lines in the water long before Sheepy let out a cowboy yip. I looked over at him. He was standing up and his rod was bent almost double. He reeled in his catch and flipped it onto the bank. It was a good-sized trout to come out of a stream. It might have been a foot long.

"It's a whopper!" said Audra.

"It's no bigger than a kid's goldfish," Walter said.

Noise carries well around water. I don't know why that is, but I could hear Audra and Sheepy talking even though they were practically whispering. I didn't mean to eavesdrop—oh, hell, yes I did—but I heard them talking about Drew.

"He ain't a bad sort," Sheepy told Audra. "Don't you never get lonesome?"

"Not that lonesome," said Audra. "I wish he'd just leave me alone. I don't encourage him any, believe me."

"Give the boy a chance."

"Quit matchmaking, Sheepy. Drew gives me the creeps. He says he's crazy in love with me, but I think he's just crazy."

Downstream from us, Betsy and Walter were talking.

"You could have been a doctor," Betsy said.

"Didn't work out so well for Rumdab, did it?"

"That's your excuse? You're afraid of being murdered if you do something with your life? I'd like to have children, but we can't as long as you're working dead-end jobs. You and your stupid inventions."

"I'll make my fortune someday."

"Sure, and I'll grow horns like a bull. I wish you'd grow up."

Upstream, Sheepy let out another yip. He started reeling in a second fish. I got a good look at it while it was flopping on the bank. A nice rainbow, almost as big as Sheepy's first catch. He worked out the hook and put the fish in his creel.

"Save some for the rest of us," I told him.

"What you using for bait?" hollered Walter. "Something besides this stupid cheese?"

"I'm using cheese," said Sheepy. "I just picked the best fishing spot. You got to learn how to read water and talk trout."

"Sure," said Walter. He reeled in his line and the cheese was gone. "Damn! Where's a worm when I need one?"

We spent about an hour fishing. Sheepy caught five nice trout. The rest of us caught nothing. Mosquitoes started buzzing around us and thunder was getting loud in the sky.

"Time for us to get going," Audra told us, standing up and reeling in her line.

"Don't worry, folks," said Sheepy, "I'll share my fish with you." He let out a cackle of a laugh.

The storm couldn't be far off. We packed up the remains of our lunch and our fishing gear and headed for the hay wagon. Sheepy and Audra broke out some worn yellow slickers for us, just in case, and we climbed back into the hay. About halfway back to the ranch, the clouds opened up and dumped a load of rain on us. The hay got wet and smelly and we sunk into it like turtles in mud. It was cold and miserable. Sheepy and Audra huddled on the wagon seat and didn't sing one song.

"Folks," Sheepy told us when we were back in front of the grub house, "there's cards and checkers to play inside. Sissy Dell and Panhandle will fix you all some coffee and hot chocolate. Enjoy your time before supper."

We all tramped into the chuck house with our straw-covered shoes and the smell of fresh coffee assaulted us.

"Want to play a game of checkers?" Walter asked me. "I invented a board game once. Kind of a cross between chess and Monopoly. It was too complicated, I guess."

"Thanks," I said, "but me and Tracy are likely headed back to our cabin. I want to think about the murder some more."

"And listen to the rain on the roof," said Tracy.

We stayed just long enough to drink some coffee and then we went out into the wet to our cabin. The roof had a leak in it and both Eben and Mayhew played with the drips.

"How are you going to find your clue?" Tracy asked me.

"As soon as the rain lets up a little, you and me

are going to go visit the crime scene. I don't suppose they'll want us out there, so we'll sneak up on the trail. We'll head straight back from the cabins until we're out of sight of the ranch buildings. Then we'll cross over to the trail."

"Why don't we go now?"

"Now? It's wet out."

"It might get worse. We've still got our slickers. You know you want to go."

"I'm tired, but you're right. Let me get my gun and flashlight. I don't suppose you packed any of those little evidence envelopes I like to carry when I'm working?"

"Of course I did. I know you."

I gathered the stuff I needed and we climbed back into our slickers. Tracy put on her cowgirl hat and I donned my sad fedora. We said goodbye to the cats—they were drinking out of the can we'd put under the drip—and went out to brave the elements.

We quickly crossed the strip of meadow behind the cabins, our shoes and pant legs collecting a lot of water, and headed into a little wooded area to the right of the trail where Rumdab had taken his fatal hike.

When we'd walked through the undergrowth beneath the trees for a while, we turned left and found the trail. We were out of sight of the ranch buildings. We kept our eyes on the trail, hoping to find something that the sheriff and his boy had missed. I'd grabbed an extra flashlight from the truck, so we had two. We found nothing.

"What are we looking for?" Tracy asked.

"Anything. The other earring, a love note, a machine gun. Anything at all that doesn't belong here."

The dirt track was still pretty dry under the trees. The hard-packed soil, covered in pine needles in lots of spots, was lousy for showing footprints. After a while, we came to the spot where the doc had been strung up. The cowboys with the badges had roped it off by tying twine to a few saplings and bushes. We ducked under the twine and spent way too much time looking for evidence that might have been missed.

"Tracy," I said, "if you'd been the murderer, how would you have gone back to the ranch?"

"I wouldn't have taken the trail, that's for sure. Too easy for somebody to come along and see me. I'd take to the woods. But it was dark. I'd want to stay as close to the trail as I could and still be able to hide in the trees."

"Right you are. I'm glad to hear you'd make a good killer."

"Something to remember if you start looking at other dames."

"Come over here under the tree where the doc was hung. Pretend it's dark and you've only got a flashlight and a weak moon to see by. Show me where you'd leave the trail to take to the woods."

She came over and stood by me and squinted her eyes to make things look dim. She was still wearing her glasses. She looked good in them. After a minute, she pointed.

"There," she said. "That bare spot. What is it, a dry creek bed?"

"Looks like." There was a rocky, twisty, path with very little vegetation except for the trees growing near it. "Why that side of the trail?"

"It's the same side that our cabins are on. I wouldn't want to have to cross the trail again. Somebody might see me. I'd walk down that creek bed a ways and then turn back towards the ranch."

"Let's do it," I said. "Keep your peepers peeled. We're looking for anything and everything."

Tracy started down the dry gulch and I followed behind her. Some rain pattered on us and the rocks under our feet were slick. Tracy walked about fifty feet and stopped.

"I think I'd start for the cabins about here."

"Do it."

We walked into a stand of low growing trees and had to duck to keep our hats from getting knocked off. At one point Tracy didn't stoop low enough and a pine bough swiped her hat. She picked it up and carried it in her fair young paw. A little farther on, she failed to duck low enough again.

"My hair!" she said.

"You can comb your lovely locks later. Wait. Hair!"

"You just noticed I was wearing some?"

"Let's go back, slowly."

"Why?"

"We're going to look for strands of hair that might have caught in the branches. If we find any, the length and color might tell us who the murderer is."

"You ought to do this for a living," said Tracy.

We backtracked. We walked very slowly, keeping an eye on the tree branches we crossed under.

"I found some," said Tracy, after we'd walked about ten yards.

I went over and looked. "It's awfully short."

"Maybe Curt was the killer."

"No, I think it's deer hair."

"Yeah?"

"Yeah. I'd say it came from a four-point buck, a good-sized fellow."

"Don't be a smart guy."

I pointed to a clump of aspen. A four-point buck stood very still, giving us the eye. Tracy spotted him and gave me an admiring look.

"OK, Davy Crockett, lead on," she said.

We spent the next twenty minutes looking for hair. I finally found a few strands tangled in the needles of some pine branches.

"Eureka!" I said.

"You found gold? Let's retire."

I carefully loosed the strands of hair. They were brown, maybe six or eight inches long. "Great! This hair could belong to you, or Audra, or Mabel, or Betsy.

"At least we've narrowed down the suspects. I don't think it's long enough for Betsy's, though it might be broken off. I think it's too light for Audra's. Can't be sure though."

I got a little yellow baby shower announcement envelope out of my pocket. Tracy wound the hair around her finger into a little curl and I put it in the envelope.

"I feel a whole lot better now," I said. "Now we've got something to go on."

"Are we going to turn this hair over to the sheriff?"

"To hell with him. He didn't find it, did he? We'll have to find a sneaky way to compare this hair to the dames at the ranch."

"Steal their hair brushes."

"Not bad. I'll leave that up to you. Let's get back to our cabin. I'm tired of being rained on. And I want to take a nap."

"A honeymoon kind of nap?"

"With you? That's exactly the kind of nap I like."

We headed back to the trail and walked it until we were just in sight of the ranch buildings. Then we headed into the woods again and made our way to our cabin. The cats sniffed us all over and showed us their empty food bowl. I filled up the bowl with their favorite smelly food and we took off our wet clothes and had our nap. It was close to suppertime when we got up.

We took a good look at the hair before we ambled — through a now misty rain — to the dining hall. Mabel was at the motel in Quail Eye. Lilly and Sissy Dell's hair was light colored. As it turned out, Audra didn't show for supper. That left Betsy as the only reasonable suspect whose hair we could get a gander at.

"I'll tell her I'm getting a bug out of her hair," said Tracy, "and I'll pull out a couple of strands."

"You'll make a shamus yet."

"Pulling hair's a big part of the job, is it?"

"You just never know. I pull mine often enough."

We went around to the back of the chow house. Panhandle was torturing a couple of big racks of ribs. Sissy Dell was fussing around, putting out plates of food and acting like there were twelve dudes instead of just four. The gloomy Walter was drinking a beer and smoking a Camel. Betsy was checking out the food and Tracy was hovering around her head.

"Is that a black widow in your hair?" Tracy asked her.

Betsy screamed. "Get it off! Get it off! Ouch!"

"Sorry," said Tracy. "His legs were tangled up in your hair. I got him though." She wiped imaginary spider remains on her pants and gave me a conspiratorial wink, pushing one hand into her pants pocket.

None of the buckaroos except Sissy Dell and Panhandle were around.

"Not much of a crowd tonight," I said, walking

up to Panhandle. He was wearing a slicker and a silly rain hat, though the rain was practically over.

"You dudes all ran away," he said. "You got yellow streaks down your backs."

"Not me and the missus. And Walter and Betsy have stuck it out. What's the plan for after supper?"

"We're all going to play hide-and-seek in the woods. Sound like fun?"

"What's the plan for real?"

"There isn't one. We're tired of trying to keep you dudes cheered up. You can all go shiver in your cabins. Maybe somebody else will get murdered."

"You've misplaced your carefree spirit," I said.

"To hell with that. I got a letter from Auntie today. She wants money for gas and the wear and tear on her car. I know what she's up to. She doesn't want me coming back."

"Were you thinking about it?"

"Hell, no. Guess what? Hester's wanting to come up here."

"I can't see her as a buckaroo."

"She won't be working here, just getting away from her boyfriends and resting up."

"How do you feel about that?"

"You know, if the only horse you can find to ride is a nag, it's still better than no horse at all."

"You and Hester are romantically involved?"

"We both got an itch, that's all," said Panhandle.

"Don't let those ribs burn."

"In the rain? I'll be lucky if I can get them cooked. Hear about Hawk?"

"I've heard nothing. What about him?"

"He went up to the big house today and quit."

"Was he scared of the killer?"

"Probably, but I think he's thinking of going back to Hollywood. Good riddance to him"

"The lady dudes will be crushed."

"You're right about that. You know, I wouldn't be surprised if Uncle Prime closed down the dude ranch. What would I do then?"

"It might help if I can find the murderer."

"How you coming along with that?"

"Give me another day or two," I said.

"For real?"

"Yeah."

Tracy joined us.

"Howdy, Mrs. Axe," said Panhandle.

"Those ribs look good." Said Tracy. "Who killed Dr. Rumdab, Panhandle?"

"I still think it was your husband here. Maybe he had a bad experience with a croaker when he was a kid."

"First I've heard of it," said Tracy. "Tell me about the bunkhouse. Do you all have one big bed or are you more private?"

"We all got our own space, like stalls in a barn. There's one bathroom and a little kitchen. I've stayed in worse flop houses."

"If one of you wanted to take a midnight stroll,

you could do it without the others knowing?" Tracy asked.

"Why you asking? You think one of the buckaroos is the killer? Hawk's leaving us. Maybe he did it."

"Answer my question." Tracy used her sternest mean waitress voice.

"Sure thing, ma'am. As long as everybody else was asleep, you could sneak out and nobody'd know."

The ribs were ready, so we helped Panhandle carry them over to the picnic tables under the veranda roof. There were scalloped potatoes, peas, biscuits, and an honest-to-God pear cactus cobbler. We'd all worked up big appetites being rained on and we did credit to the meal. Afterwards, Panhandle unlimbered his guitar and Sissy Dell crooned some cowboy songs. Tom Dooley wasn't one of them.

"You still looking for a checkers partner?" I asked Walter.

"No. Panhandle beat me about twelve games this afternoon."

"Did you play for money?"

"Yeah. Don't tell Betsy. Any luck with solving the murder?"

"Nothing I can talk about, but Tracy and me got our clue."

"You guys are good. I hope they hang the guy like they did Rumdab."

"They gas folks in Colorado," I said.

"Hanging'd be better."

Not if the killer is your wife, I thought.

"Let's play some cards," Tracy suggested.

"I think me and Walter are just going to stay in our cabin tonight," said Betsy. "We're not feeling too cheery."

"Why sulk in your cabin? Me and Axe will cheer you up. How about some Canasta?"

"I've got to work on my new invention," said Walter. "It's a new kind of saddle, with handlebars. Sorry, me and Betsy aren't much for cards anyway."

"Spoil sports," I said. "I guess we'll see you for breakfast then."

"Sure," said Walter, "if we're all still alive."

They got up, thanked Sissy Dell and Panhandle for the supper, and crept off to their cabin.

"I want to talk to Sissy Dell for a minute," Tracy told me. "I want to know if anyone's been slipping out of the bunkhouse at night."

"OK. You want me to join you?"

"No, a guy would just screw it up."

Tracy went off to help Sissy Dell carry things into the kitchen. I went to help Panhandle clean up.

"Thanks," he told me, when I picked up a stack of plates. "You still think me and Ned worked together to swipe Auntie's bunny?"

"I'm not sure what I think. You could be innocent. Stranger things have happened."

14

In a few minutes, Tracy rejoined me and we headed to our cabin. She couldn't wait to compare the hairs she'd plucked from Betsy to the ones we'd found in the woods.

"How'd you make out with Sissy Dell?" I asked.

"She was a bust. She says she sleeps like the dead. Bad choice of words, considering."

When we got back to the cabin, we found the cats had been busy in our absence. They'd amused themselves by trying to unhook the hooked rug on the floor. They'd made pretty good progress and I figured the ranch would bill us for the damage. Tracy took the hairs from the evidence envelope and compared them to the ones she'd plucked from Betsy. She frowned. "Betsy's not our killer. Her hair is about the right shade, but it's thicker. These hairs don't match at all."

"That leaves Mabel and Audra, or someone we don't even know about. I'm going to hide those hairs we found in case somebody searches our place."

"You're awfully suspicious."

"That's an attitude that pays off. Where should I hide them?"

"Tape them to one of the cats."

"Maybe not. I could stick them to a bar of soap if we had a bathroom in here."

"Why don't you just keep them in your pocket? They aren't heavy."

"I think that's what I'll do. Listen, figure out a way to get some of Audra's hair. You can't use the bug ploy again. I don't think Audra is afraid of bugs. She was playing with a couple of ants the other day, trying to get them to race."

"I'll think of something," said Tracy. "Don't worry, partner."

"You did good today."

"Thanks, chief."

"Panhandle told me his so-called cousin Hester is coming up to the dude ranch. I wonder how's she's going to ride a horse with those slinky dresses she wears."

"Maybe they can find a side saddle for her."

"She's trouble. I'm sorry she's coming up here."

"She can help us pass the long rainy days," said Tracy.

"If you think Betsy's a flirt, wait until you see Hester in action. She makes Betsy look like a bashful nun."

"Oh, in that case we need to put a padlock on

Hester's cabin door. But you don't get to keep the key."

"She's not a looker."

"That's good news."

It rained all night. We couldn't even take the cats out for an airing. I felt like pacing so I did. Tracy didn't like it.

"Go outside if you're going to pace. You're making the cats nervous."

"I'll get wet."

"It'll do you good. Your clothes need washing anyway," said Tracy.

"If you're going to be a detective you'll have to learn how to pace."

"Remind me to practice sometime later. I'll go for a walk with you right now, though."

"We'll catch our deaths."

"Around here, that could be true."

We struggled into the baggy yellow slickers the ranch had loaned us and went outside. It was cold and damp and dark. I tried lighting a cigar but the rain kept putting it out. The lights were out in Betsy and Walter's cabin.

"There's still lights on in the dining hall," said Tracy. "Let's go see if they have any coffee, or whiskey."

"No whiskey. We're on the clock."

"Maybe you're on the clock, but I'm on vacation. I'll get drunk as a hoot owl if I want."

We sloshed up to the grub house. The door was unlocked and Panhandle was inside. He turned to look at us.

"Sleep walking?" he asked. He was putting tablecloths on the tables, and lining up the benches and chairs. "I got to get as much done as I can for breakfast tomorrow or Sissy Dell will kill me."

"Why?" asked Tracy, shaking the water off of her like a dog.

"I got to drive down to Quail Eye and pick up my cousin at the bus stop in the morning. I won't be here to help cook."

"What are you going to drive?" I asked.

"I'll borrow the ranch truck."

"Is your cousin Hester related to your uncle Prime?" Tracy asked Panhandle.

"Damned if I know. I know they've never met. You guys want some coffee?"

"Sure, if you've got," I said.

"Have you got a drop of whiskey to put in it?" asked Tracy.

Panhandle raised his considerable eyebrows. "Sure, sister, I've got a bottle in the pantry."

"Tracy's been working with me," I said. "She thinks she's a tough guy detective now. Pretty soon she'll be smoking cigars and carrying her own gun."

"And I want my own blackjack, and my own fedora."

"The whole gumshoe mystique is going to her head," I explained to Panhandle. "Be careful she doesn't sock you on the jaw."

Panhandle shrugged and went into the kitchen.

169

In a minute, he came back carrying a big metal tray with a coffee pot and cups and a pint of whiskey on it. Tracy and me shrugged out of our slickers and sat at one of the tables. Panhandle joined us.

"Just coffee's fine for me, thanks," I said.

Panhandle poured out our coffee. He added a dollop of hooch to his and Tracy's cups.

"There's some cookies in the kitchen if you want," said Panhandle.

"None for me," I said.

"I'm still full from supper," said Tracy.

"OK, you guys," said Panhandle, "spill. Who killed the little doc?"

"He was killed by a horse. I think it was Lucky." I said.

Panhandle snorted. "Even I know better than that. Come on, who?"

"We don't know yet," I said, "but we've got some ideas. We're keeping them close to the vest for now."

"How well do you know Audra?" Tracy asked Panhandle.

Damn Tracy and her big mouth.

"Audra, huh?" Panhandle's eyebrows practically jumped off his face. "You think that short stack of sweet flapjacks strangled the croaker? I don't see it."

"We need some of her hair," said Tracy. "Just a few strands."

"You guys making voodoo dolls or something?"

"Never mind my partner," I said. "She talks too much. Tracy admires Audra's hair and is thinking of having a wig made. She needs a sample to take to her wig maker."

"Sure," said Panhandle.

"It's true," said Tracy. "I have a lot of wigs. I'm wearing one right now. You'd never know, would you?"

Panhandle made a disgusted noise. "Why can't you two be straight with me? I might be able to help."

"We're just kicking some ideas around," I said, "that's all. If we think we can use your help, we'll fill you in on the details." I changed the subject. "What time is Hester arriving?"

"I'm picking her up at seven. I hope to hell she doesn't bring all her clothes with her. I don't feel like hoisting suitcases. You looking forward to seeing her again, cousin Miles?"

"Why not? She's OK. A little over-friendly maybe."

He snorted. "Only with guys. She hates broads. You want some of Audra's hair? Maybe Hester will get in a catfight with her. That'll make the hair fly."

"You arrange the fight," said Tracy. "I'll bring my butterfly net."

"It sounds like Hester and Betsy won't get along," I said.

"You're right about that," said Panhandle.

"Hester don't like competition. I figure those two will get into it. Care to lay any bets about which one has the best right hook?"

"I'd put my money on Hester," I said. "She's a flyweight, but there's always blood in her eye."

"You folks ought to go to bed," said Panhandle. "Tomorrow's going to be a big day."

"Why is that?" asked Tracy. "Are we riding elephants tomorrow?"

"No. They're taking you dudes to the Lost Buckaroo Mine."

"Is it dangerous?" I asked.

"You better hope not. They've shored it up with new timbers, but most of it's an actual cave. They tapped into it when they were blasting out the mineshafts. You'll love it."

"We're going to ride horses into a cave?" asked Tracy.

"Naw, you'll leave the horses outside. They'll give you miner's hats—you know, with lights on them—and you'll walk and crawl. Don't wear your best duds. It's muddy, and rocky, and slimy."

"Sounds swell," I said.

"It's worth the trouble," said Panhandle. "There's big rooms full of those dangly things—stalactites—and crystals, and blind fish. It's better than a drive-in movie."

"I'm getting excited," said Tracy. "Any animals? Blind albino bears? Giant salamanders?"

"No, but there's supposed to be a ghost. A miner was blown up when they discovered the cave. He haunts the place."

"How's come this wasn't in the brochure?" I asked. "It sounds creepier than hell."

"It's new this year. Like I said, they had to shore up the old mine shafts. Someday they're going to put electricity in the cave. Lights all over. Only now, I guess, that might not happen if Uncle Prime shuts down the whole dude ranch."

"Have you thought what you might do?" asked Tracy.

Panhandle sighed. "Beats me. Maybe I'll stay on as a Twin Roans ranch hand. It's getting late. You guys should go to bed."

"You trying to get rid of us?" I asked.

"One more cup of coffee," said Tracy. "With another shot of whiskey."

Panhandle looked at me. "Some dame you married."

"There's none better," I said.

We drank our coffee and then headed back to our cabin. We played with the cats a little and then hit the sack.

"Tomorrow's going to be some day," said Tracy. "Cousin Hester and a cave. What do you think?"

"I could do without either one of them. Don't forget about Audra's hair. Grab a sample the first chance you get. But don't let her catch you doing it."

"I'll borrow some mule shears from the barn."

Somewhere near dawn, I woke up. Light was just beginning to pale the sky. I had the impression that something, some sound, had awakened me. I wasn't wrong. Something thumped against the outside of our door. It was more a clunk than a knock. I thought maybe some animal was paying us a visit, maybe to get to our cats. There was another thunk, a little louder. It woke Tracy.

"What's going on?" she asked.

"I don't know. Let me check."

I snagged my snub-nose from under the pillow and got out of bed. I crept to the door and crouched to one side of it. Flipping on the porch light, I opened the door a crack. Tracy followed me, the idiot. There was the sound of breaking glass, and an explosion. A gunshot!

"Get down!" I shouted. I turned and pulled Tracy with me to the floor. There was a second shot. I heard the bullet hit the wall above our bed. "Stay down!"

I was afraid the sniper might get closer to the cabin and continue shooting. I alligator-crawled to the window and then raised up just enough to look over the sill. I opened the window a few inches and fired a couple of shots into the sky and then listened. Nothing. Not a sound. I waited for more shots, but there weren't any. Tracy crawled over to me.

"Get away from that window," she said.

One of the cats started mewing, but he didn't sound hurt. Tracy and me stayed on the floor for what seemed like an hour. It was probably more like ten minutes. Then I heard rapid footsteps outside. There was a hard knock at the door.

"Mr. and Mrs. Hatchett! Are you all right?"

It was Breedlaw. I climbed up off the floor and opened the door. Breedlaw, looking rumpled, even a little drunk, was standing on our doorstep. He had a rifle in his hands.

"We're fine," I told him. "Somebody shot a couple of holes through our window. No real harm done."

"By God! What's this place coming to? Did you see the shooter?"

"Naw, not enough light, and I was too busy hugging the floor."

"Who do you think it was?" Breedlaw asked.

"I was hoping you had some ideas. Maybe it was Rumdab's killer. Is everyone accounted for? Did the shots wake everybody up?"

"I think so. Folks were piling out of the bunkhouse. I don't guess Walter and Betsy woke up though. Their cabin is quiet."

"Maybe they're laying low. How'd you know me and Tracy were the ones being shot at?"

"I saw your porch light was on, and then I saw the broken window. I'm going to go call the sheriff."

"Don't. No point in getting him out of bed, he can't do anything. Who knows? Maybe it was just some deer poacher getting an early start. Two of the shots were mine. I think I hit a cloud. Listen,

Breedlaw, I'd appreciate it if you kept this under your Stetson. I've got my reasons. Tell the others I heard a bear outside and took some pot shots at it."

"No," said Tracy. She'd pulled on a robe and followed me to the door. "Tell everybody I'm the one who fired the shots. That will be more believable. Silly dame and all that. I even managed to shoot a hole through my own window. I'm just one of those dizzy, skittish, broads. Do you think you can tell that story?"

Breedlaw looked like he didn't know what to do. He decided to take the easy way out.

"All right," he said. "I don't like it, but I don't like bringing the sheriff back up here either. We'll just let sleeping dogs lie. Whoever fired the shots was after you, I figure. No point in spooking the buckaroos or the other guests. I'll tell folks your misses went bear hunting."

"Thanks," I said.

Breedlaw left. Tracy and me got dressed after first checking the cats for bullet holes. They were unventilated, thank God.

"Why do you want to keep the shooting a secret?" Tracy asked.

"I don't know. Maybe I'm just tired of looking at badges. Besides, it occurs to me that the sniper might be the same idiot who shot at me in my office. Ned. I kept an eye out for him on our drive to the ranch. I didn't spot his truck, but he might be in communication with Panhandle. I want to handle Ned all by myself. No cops."

"You're stupid and stubborn."

"Stop sweet-talking me, you'll make me blush. You know, you could have caught one of those bullets. Are you sure marrying a detective was a good idea?"

"Sure. I want to be a gumshoe, too. It's exciting. We'll just both have to start wearing armor. Look on the bright side, at least this time nobody put holes in your hat."

I checked the damage to our window. One pane in the latticed window had been shot to pieces. I was afraid the cats might climb up on the sill and make their escape; They'd been pretty impressed with the outdoors. I took a couple of my shirts from our suitcase and balled them up to stuff into the unglazed hole. That would have to do for now.

When we went to breakfast the next morning, the sun was shining. It figures, since we were going to spend the day underground. We ate our flapjacks with Betsy and Walter. Sheepy's five trout also made an appearance. They were delicious. Betsy was goggle-eyed about Tracy's having shot at a real live bear.

"Tracy, honey, weren't you scared?" Betsy asked.

"Naw, it wasn't too big a bear, maybe five-hundred pounds."

"You never even saw the thing," I said. "I'm guessing it was a muskrat."

"It sounded like a horse walking around," said

Tracy. "I'll bet that bear was bigger than you, Axe."

"I'll bet it smelled worse than me."

"Oh, yeah? Is that likely?"

"Do you think you wounded it?" Betsy asked. "I've heard wounded bears are the most dangerous. Or hungry ones, or ones with cubs."

"Or naturally grouchy ones," I said. "Or one's whose shoes hurt them."

Walter put in his oar. "I think the kind that have lost money on Wall Street are the hardest to get along with."

"I don't see how you two boys can laugh about it," complained Betsy. "You're probably just jealous. What'd you do when you heard the bear, Axe, hide under the bed?"

"Absolutely. With my favorite stuffed bunny wrapped in my arms."

"Quit making fun of Tracy," said Betsy. She looked almost fierce. "I could never be that brave. If I wake up in the night and hear something, I always make Walter investigate."

"Boy, that's the truth," said Walter, rolling his eyes. "If a mouse so much as licks its lips in the night, Betsty's wanting me to grab the hatchet and go look."

Sissy Dell came around to refill our coffee cups.

"Brave girl," she told Tracy.

Breedlaw wandered into the chow house. He looked hung-over, and his mustache drooped. He winked at Tracy.

"'Morning, Daniel Boone," he said to Tracy, grinning like a loon. "Say, is it true you can shoot out a squirrel's eye at fifty paces?"

"No," said Tracy, "but I can spit in your eye from right where I'm sitting."

Breedlaw retreated.

We quit talking and concentrated on shoveling grub into our craws. Walter could pack away the pancakes like a starving stevedore. I didn't do so bad myself.

"Let me tell you folks about the cave you're going to see today," Sissy Dell told us "It's beautiful. There's this one big room with shiny crystals all over the walls. There's an echo chamber, and a little lake with fish that can't see, poor things. They're white and scrawny. You might even meet up with the ghost of Blasty Graber. He was the one who blew the hole through the mine wall that revealed the cave. But he dynamited himself to death in the process, poor fellow."

"Yeah, poor blown up Blasty," said Walter. "And poor little blind fish. Caves give me the screaming meemies. Can't we just ride horses?"

"You'll get to do that too," said Sissy Dell, her smile like a slice of sunshine. "There's way more flapjacks, bacon, eggs, and toast. Eat up folks!"

We finished up our breakfast and went outside. Sheepy, Drew, and Audra had our string of horses saddled up and waiting. An old green pickup was coming up the road. The driver honked a couple of times and speeded up.

"That must be Panhandle and Hester," I told Tracy.

"Hester will be just in time to join us for the ride and the cave exploring," she said.

"Swell," I said. "I wonder if she's wearing high heels and a tight skirt."

The two got out of the truck. Panhandle looked grumpy. Hester was smiling. She was dressed in new, too-tight, jeans, a fancy pink cowgirl shirt with too many buttons unfastened, and new red cowboy boots. On her head was a tiny pink cowboy hat with a veil on the brim. I wondered where she got the money for the outfit, but I didn't really want to know.

15

"I'll put your bags in the cabin," Panhandle told her. "You've got cabin number one. I'll leave the key in the dining hall. Get moving, these folks are waiting on you."

Hester came forward and introduced herself to Walter.

"Howdy! My name's Hester, what's yours?"

Her long dark hair was fluffed out and she hadn't skimped on the makeup. She was lean and lanky and pale as a blind fish. Her long face had a big smile plastered on it.

"I'm Betsy." Walter's wife stepped between him and Hester and staked out her territory. "You must have dressed in a hurry, honey, you missed a couple of buttons."

"I'm Tracy," said my girl, stepping forward to stave off the fireworks. "This is my husband, Axe."

Hester batted her fake lashes at me and gave me an up-from-under smoldering glance. If I'd had a bucket of water handy I would have used it on her.

"We've met," she said. "Only he wasn't named Axe the night I spent with him."

"I'm still trying out names," I said. "I didn't spend the whole night with you, Hester, it only seemed like it. How are you?"

"Raring to go, sweetie. Let me at those horses."

Audra gave Hester an appraising look. I don't figure she thought the pink-hatted damsel would fetch much at a flea market.

"Do you know how to ride?" Audra asked Hester.

"I can ride a bicycle. Does that count?"

"It's not quite the same," said Audra. "If you need any help, let me or Drew know. That's what we're here for.

We climbed into our various saddles and the guides led us up a trail we hadn't traveled before. Audra had her shotgun with her and Sheepy and Drew both wore gun belts. I couldn't help wondering if either of their shooting irons had been fired recently. Like last night, maybe. Drew had cleaned up some. He was wearing a fancy turquoise shirt and was attempting a mustache. He still looked like a new-born calf with pimples. I wondered if he was trying to take over Hawk's spot as a lady killer.

I had my High Power tucked into my belt and Tracy had my little thirty-eight stuck in her jean's pocket. She'd insisted on carrying it. If a whole posse of killers showed up, we'd be ready.

Hester couldn't follow the rules. We were supposed to ride single file, but she kept urging her horse — a hammer-headed gray — up next to Drew. She batted all of her eyelashes at him, shook her tiny bosom, and generally made a nuisance of herself. Audra kept telling her to get back in line but Hester ignored her. Audra's face began turning the color of the sorrel pony she was riding, and her nostrils flared.

"I just love a cowboy," Hester gushed at Drew. "So manly and romantic."

"Thank you, ma'am," Drew almost stammered. "I'm not much of a cowboy, though. I can scarce rope a steer."

"I'm sure you have other talents," breathed Hester, leaning toward the poor boy and almost falling out of her saddle.

"We're supposed to be riding single-file, ma'am," said Drew. "Like Audra said."

"Oh, who listens to little old Audra?" simpered Hester. "It's so much cozier riding by your side. Is that a real gun?"

"Yes, ma'am, but I don't aim to shoot it."

Audra had had enough.

"Drew!" she called. "Ride on up ahead and make sure that bear Mrs. Hatchett shot at last night ain't waiting for us."

Drew, happy to get away, spurred his mount and trotted up the trail, sans Hester.

Audra grabbed Hester's horse's bridle. "You

ride behind. We got rules on this ranch."

Hester protested. "But I want to hear about the bear."

"Later," Audra told her.

Hester sulked, but waited for the rest of us to pass her so she could dine on our dust.

We clung to our cayuses up a winding trail that was half mud, the horse's hooves slipping. I thought one of us was sure to fall off, but it didn't happen. Audra made us sing cowboy songs, but Hester insisted on crooning every one of them like they were torch songs. Her voice was husky, sultry, and completely off key. Audra finally told us all we'd done enough singing for one day. Around noon, we rode into a clearing backed by a big pile of boulders. Amidst the rocks the squared timbers of an old mine entrance showed.

We all climbed off our horses. Sheepy made a hitch rail by stretching a rope between two trees. He tied up our nags for us. He stayed outside to watch the livestock while the rest of us stacked our cowboy hats on some big rocks and donned miner's hats that Drew and Audra passed out to us. The little tin hats had battery-powered lights on their fronts. We switched them on.

"Everybody stay close and stay together," Audra told us. "We don't want anybody wandering off and getting lost."

I saw Tracy unwrapping some bubble gum. She put three pieces into her ample mouth and started chewing. She gave me a wink. I had no idea what the hell she was up to.

"Watch where you step," Drew told us. "There's water dripping from the roof and the floors are nothing but loose gravel."

We lined up in single file. Tracy bumped me with her shoulder and headed up behind Audra. I followed along. Hester took her place behind Drew, and Walter and Betsy brought up the rear. The mineshaft sloped downward and snaked all over the place. The rough rock ceiling was partly held up with timbers hewn from entire tree trunks. The place was a good ten degrees cooler than the outside. We plodded along like blind snails and every so often Audra stopped us to point out some feature of interest. A streak of gold ore, some mica, a natural rock shaped like a duck's head. After a time we came to a blacker spot in the darkness. Our lights showed us a ragged hole with some cold air coming out of it.

"This here's the cave entrance," Audra explained. "This old mine had a nice vein of gold, but it played out. This hole they blasted was a last effort to find more gold. Blasty the miner was killed here. Keep your eyes peeled for his ghost. We're going to enter the cave now. The ceiling's low and there's spots where we've stretched ropes to keep you from stepping off into big holes. Be careful, dudes. Don't even think about straying from the trail.

We followed Audra and Drew, Tracy smacking her bubble gum and practically stepping on Audra's heels. She blew a big bubble and popped it. I thought her cave manners could use some improving. We ducked under stalactites, clamored over stalagmites, brushed against clammy walls, all the time shining our headlights around. At one point, the cave opened up into a pretty good-sized cavern, and there were some kind of quartz crystals all over the walls. They winked and glimmered in our lights and put on quite a show. Audra stopped us so we could appreciate the underground jewels.

"Keep close together now, folks," Audra told us. "We're getting close to the spot where Blasty likes to show up. You'll know him by his long white beard."

"Maybe he's really Santa," said Walter.

"Laugh if you want," said Audra, "but I'm telling you, the ghost is real. I've seen him myself."

Hester squealed and pressed herself against Drew.

"What happens if we pull on his beard?" I asked.

"I wouldn't," said Audra. "Blasty carries a big Colt revolver. He might shoot your tin hat off."

We crossed the big cavern and entered another tunnel. Water dripped all over us. A cold breeze blew in from somewhere.

"Is there another entrance to the cave?" asked Betsy. "Where's that air coming from?"

"Nobody's ever found another entrance," said Drew. "We've looked. There's no telling how that wind gets in here."

The rough tunnel wound around and finally came out into a low-ceilinged room as dark as Satan's eyebrows.

"Turn out your lights, dudes," said Audra. "Some of the rocks in here glow in the dark."

We reluctantly switched off our miner's lights. The place stayed dark. Then, over in a corner, an eerie green light appeared. It started moving towards us. All at once, the light grew brighter and we were looking at the haggard, bearded, face of a walking corpse. Somebody screamed in a high-pitched squeal. I think it was me.

"Howdy, folks!" the ghost greeted us. It pulled off its silly beard and grinned like a loon. It was that damned Panhandle. Somehow he'd managed to beat us to the cave, probably riding by a shortcut. "You keep looking for the ghost of Blasty, cause you ain't found him yet."

He laughed. We all laughed. It was a great joke. None of us had been scared. Of course not. We turned our headlamps back on. I realized I was holding my pistol. I looked at Tracy. My thirty-eight was in her paw. Something gleamed to my right and I looked that way. Walter was clutching a nickel-plated pistol in one hand.

"I almost made you a real ghost," Walter told Panhandle.

"You almost made me pee myself, Billy," complained Hester.

"Just a little joke, folks," Panhandle said, nervously. He pulled a flashlight with a green bulb out of his shirt and switched it off. His hands were shaking.

"Let's everybody put up their hardware," said Drew. "We was just having a little fun."

We filed into another tunnel. Tracy kept smacking her gum and blowing bubbles. What was wrong with her? After fifty yards or so, we came into a low cavern whose floor glimmered in our lights.

"This here's the lake," said Audra. "Don't fall in. It's said to be half a mile deep. Look for the blind fish."

We all looked into the water. I saw something swimming around, something white and wriggly. They were fish all right. I wondered if they were really blind, or just faking it so we'd give them treats.

"This here's as far as we go," said Drew. "We'll head back and have us a picnic lunch in front of the mine. You see any gold nuggets on the floor; you're welcome to pick them up."

On our way out Tracy stumbled and bumped into Audra.

"I'm so sorry, Audra!" she said. "I tripped. I was blowing a bubble and I got gum in your hair. Let me pull it out."

Smart girl!

"You got gum in my hair?" complained Audra. "Get it out, but be careful. I don't want to be bald."

Tracy got the pink bubble gum out, no doubt with a few strands of hair stuck to it. I saw her wrap it up in a piece of paper and put it in her pocket.

We filed out of the cave and back into the mine. In a little while, we were back outdoors. A nice lunch of barbequed beef sandwiches was waiting for us. Panhandle joined us. His face and hands were covered with flour. He came over to where me and Tracy were sitting in the grass.

"You could have shot me," he complained.

"I was just fooling," I said. "Whose idea was it to have you play ghost?"

"Breedlaw's. You wouldn't expect him to have a funny bone, but he does."

"Where's your horse?" asked Tracy.

"Over in the trees. I beat you guys here by about ten minutes." He leaned over near Tracy. "You got any more bubble gum?"

"Why, do you need a haircut?"

"That was a pretty neat trick."

"Tracy shrugged. "Just normal detective stuff."

"You think Audra bumped off the doc?" whispered Panhandle.

"Maybe, maybe not. We'll soon know."

"What do you think of my cousin Hester?"

"She looks just like you," said Tracy.

"Like hell she does."

"She's a pistol," I said, joining in on the conspiratorial conversation. "I wonder what Drew thinks of her."

"I hope he likes her," said Panhandle. "Drew could use a girlfriend and Audra won't have anything to do with him. Besides, you're putting her behind bars."

"Keep that under your hat. We're a long ways from proving Audra did anything at all," I said.

We stuffed ourselves full of lunch, piled onto our broncs, and headed back to the ranch. On the way, it started to rain. When we finally reached the barn, we all went to the grub house for coffee. Tracy was fidgety and I could tell she wanted to go back to our cabin. I hoped maybe she was feeling romantic, but that wasn't it. As soon as we got back to our place, she asked me for my hair sample. She eagerly compared it to Audra's, which still had some pink gum stuck to it.

"It's the same," said Tracy, after close examination. "The hair we found in the woods is Audra's. Same color, same texture, same length. She murdered Dr. Rumdab."

"Prove it."

"What? How?" She gave me her confused walrus look.

"Exactly my thought. We'll have to wring a confession out of her. We need to know her motive. Without knowing that, we've got nothing. The sheriff will laugh at us."

"Then let's get busy figuring out a way to trick Audra into confessing."

"Couldn't we get some sleep first?"

"Not until we have a plan."

"Fine," I said, "here's the plan. We need to talk to Lilly. If Audra killed Lilly's husband it was for a reason, and nothing that's happened at the dude ranch would provide enough of a motive. Audra knew Rumdab, but he didn't know her. That's the only thing that makes sense. Something happened in the past to make her hate him."

"Enough to kill him. So why didn't she kill him sooner?"

"Maybe she didn't have the opportunity. The doctor showed up at the Carefree Buckaroo, then Brice was killed, apparently murdered. It made a perfect setup for Audra. She could wreak her revenge on Rumdab and then blame the death on Jack the Roper. Made to order. She wouldn't have known at first that Brice hanged himself."

"I like it. Let's go talk to Lilly."

"We'll go visit her in the morning. I'm assuming she's still staying at a motel in Quail Eye. Panhandle can tell us where she is."

"Tomorrow?"

"Sure. We've got thing to do before dinner."

"Like what?"

"Like taking a nap."

"Oh," said Tracy. "I'm suddenly very sleepy." And she grinned.

At breakfast next morning, Hester showed up in silk pajamas, a kimono, and marabou slippers. But her hair was combed and her makeup was painted on just so.

"It's too early to be awake," Hester complained.

191

"Do cowboys really get up this early?"

Panhandle was putting a platter of bacon on the buffet table. "Cowboys get up when the cows do. Get used to it, cousin. You aren't going riding in that outfit, are you?"

"I'll change in time."

"What's the plan for today?" Betsy asked. She was sitting between Hester and Walter, as immovable as the Rock of Gibraltar.

"You're going to ride up to an old ghost town," said Sissy Dell, who was busy refilling all of our coffee cups.

"Sounds like fun," said Tracy, "but me and Axe were thinking of driving down and visiting Curt and Mabel."

"That so?" said Panhandle. "I didn't know you guys were such friends."

"Sure. We feel kind of sorry for them being stuck in town. Where are they staying, do you know?"

"There's only one motel in Quail Eye," said Sissy Dell. "The Sleepy Eye. Tell them hey from us."

"You got it."

"Why not wait until after we see the ghost town?" Betsy asked. "Gee, I'd hate for you to miss it."

"I think Curt and Mabel have plans later in the day," I said. "Maybe me and Tracy will ride up to the ghost town on our own sometime."

"Just the two of you?" asked Walter, looking gloomy as usual. "There's safety in numbers you know."

"Yeah," said Tracy, "but Axe and me are two tough hombres."

Walter shrugged. "Suit yourselves."

We filled our bellies, said goodbye to our fellow dudes, and headed out to the truck. Panhandle had told us the motel was on the east edge of town. We couldn't miss it. We drove down the rutted roads, stirring up a lot of dust, and made Quail Eye about nine o'clock.

"We should have called ahead," said Tracy. "They might be out to breakfast or something.

"Then we'll wait for them. I don't like giving folks any warning when I want to talk to them. I like to take them by surprise."

"Lilly's got nothing to hide."

"We don't know that. Maybe she knows why Audra might have wanted Lilly's husband dead but doesn't want to talk about it. Maybe there's some scandal involved."

"What if she doesn't know anything?"

"Then we will have wasted our time. Welcome to the detective business, precious."

16

The Sleepy Eye was a row of flat-roofed cottages painted pink and aqua. The aqua was to let you know that they had a swimming pool. I don't know what the pink was for. Both Curt and Mabel's, and Lilly's cars were parked in front of cottages.

"Looks like everybody's home," I said.

"We should have brought a hostess gift."

We were just getting out of the truck when one of the cottage doors opened and Curt and Mabel appeared. They went next door and knocked. We joined them. They seemed genuinely happy to see us.

"Hey, you two!" said Mabel. "What brings you to Quail Eye? Are you going to be staying here? Has there been another murder?"

"No," I said, "everything at the Carefree Buckaroo is hunky dory. We just thought we'd visit you folks, see how things are going."

"We're doing fine," said Curt. "We were just

picking up Lilly to go to breakfast. I guess you two have already eaten."

Tracy poked a discreet elbow into my ribs. "We overslept this morning. We missed breakfast. We'd be happy to join you guys."

"The more the merrier," said Mabel. "We could all go in one car. Why isn't Lilly answering our knock?"

Just then Lilly's door opened. She was dressed too fancy for breakfast in Quail Eye.

"Look whose joining us," Mabel said to Lilly. "Tracy and Axe just dropped by to see us."

Lilly's smile faded for a moment, but she got it back on her face in time to greet us. "The detective and his wife," she said.

"We're just civilians today," said Tracy. "Mind if we join you for breakfast?"

"That'd be lovely. We're going right now."

We all piled into Curt and Mabel's Chrysler and Curt drove us to a busy restaurant called the Hungry Bird. Inside was a smell of bacon grease and maple syrup, and the noise of clashing cutlery. The waitress — a gnome with improbable red hair — seated us in a booth and brought us water and coffee. I looked at the well-thumbed menu. I wasn't exactly hungry but, what the hell? I ordered scrambled eggs, sausage, and French toast. The conversation started out pretty general. I waited for an opportunity to bring up the murder. It occurred to me that Curt and Mabel and Lilly didn't know that Brice Holcombe wasn't a murder victim.

"Some rain we're having," observed Curt. "You getting any in the mountains?"

"Sure," said Tracy. "They've got us riding water buffalo now. What have you guys been finding to do?"

"Well," said Mabel, "we went to the Quarter Horse Museum yesterday, and we played some miniature golf. Then we went back to the motel and played cards."

"We took a hayride in the rain," said Tracy. "And we went and saw a cave."

"There were blind fish," I said, trying to make them envious.

"I'd like to go home," said Lilly. She sighed.

"They still won't let you leave, huh?" I asked.

"No. We're supposed to talk to the sheriff today. I can't believe they consider me a suspect."

Our food came and we shoveled it into our craws like happy birds.

"The sooner they find the murderer, the sooner you can go home," Tracy told Lilly.

"Do you have any idea who the killer might be?" Curt asked me.

"I've got some ideas."

"We have some ideas," Tracy corrected me.

"Apparently," I said, "Brice, the wrangler, killed himself. There's been only one actual murder."

I let them digest that along with their eggs.

"Really?" asked Curt, chewing.

"That's right."

Lilly had stopped eating. She stared at me a moment. "Did my husband's killer know that the wrangler was a suicide?"

"I doubt it," I said. "It looks like it was a copy-cat killing—an attempt to take away suspicion from your husband's actual murderer. Of course, this means we aren't dealing with a random killer, somebody who does it for fun. Dr. Rumdab goes on vacation and someone decides to do him in. Why? He couldn't have made an enemy that fast."

"He wasn't—polite," said Lilly. "but that's hardly a justification for killing him."

Her eyes were puffy under her makeup. She looked worn out and beaten down.

"Is there any chance your husband knew someone at the ranch?" I asked her. "Somebody from his past maybe?"

"No. He would have told me, and he didn't. Besides, he didn't have any enemies, not really. He rubbed a couple of colleagues the wrong way, back home. That happens in the medical profession. But why would some cowboy want him dead?"

"A former patient maybe?" I asked. "I mean, I'm not saying they'd have any actual reason to hate him, but you know how sick people are sometimes. Maybe he failed to cure somebody and a relative felt he hadn't done everything he could. Something like that."

Lilly thought about it. "Sometimes patients die.

It's not the doctor's fault, but sometimes they blame him."

"Did that happen with your husband?" asked Tracy.

"A couple of times. Of course, he found it hard to deal with. Such things are so unfair. Think of all the people whose lives he saved. I always told him to remember that. I hope it helped."

"So," I said, "a couple of his patients died and the survivors blamed him? Do you remember anything about those cases? I mean, it might be important. It could be there's someone at the dude ranch whose relative or friend was your husband's patient. It could happen."

"I suppose," said Lilly, looking thoughtful. "There was this man — a beast, really — who sued Karl for malpractice. Karl had diagnosed the man as having hemorrhoids. It turned out he had a brain tumor."

"Any doctor could make that kind of mistake," I said.

"Yes. Then, there was the orphan girl."

"The orphan girl?" Tracy asked.

"Her father had died young. Her mother came down with a malady that puzzled Karl. He tried everything he could think of to cure her. Finally he advised surgery. He thought it might be her kidneys. The surgeon found nothing, but the patient died on the operating table. She likely had something wrong with her heart.

"The surgeon, the scoundrel, tried to blame

Karl for the woman's death. And I'm afraid the poor woman's child believed the surgeon. She wrote Karl letters for months. Nothing came of it. But the girl—I believe she was around fifteen, ended up in some kind of orphanage. She was convinced that her mother would have lived if it hadn't been for my husband's diagnosis. She felt her life had been ruined by Karl."

"What was the girl's name?" I asked. "Do you remember?"

"No. It happened before Karl and I were married, but he sometimes talked about it."

"Interesting," I said. "So I guess the kid eventually stopped writing Dr. Rumdab?"

"Apparently, yes."

"Have you told the cops about this?" asked Tracy.

"Why would I? I didn't even think about it. I hardly think it likely that someone at the Carefree Buckaroo had any connection with my husband. Why wouldn't Karl remember the person's name?"

"Maybe the girl changed her name for some reason," I said. "Maybe she's using a nickname. Who knows?"

Tracy and I exchanged a look. No doubt we were both wondering if Audra was an orphan.

By the time I finished my second breakfast, I felt liked a taxidermied quail. Then we went back to the motel.

"We were thinking of taking in a movie later,"

Mabel told me and Tracy when we were saying goodbye in the parking lot. "Quail Eye has a drive in. Would you two care to join us?"

"What's the film?" I asked.

"Revenge of the Space Lizards."

"Wouldn't you know it," I said, regretfully, "me and Tracy just saw that one in the theater."

We said our goodbyes — Tracy hugged Lilly — and got into our truck.

"Now what?" Tracy asked, as we hit the road.

"We find out if Audra is an orphan and we confront her with Rumdab's murder."

"What if she denies it?"

"You could try your bubble gum trick again. That might make her confess."

When we got back to the Carefree Buckaroo, we were the only dudes in sight. Hester, Betsy, and Walter were still apparently at the ghost town.

"I would have liked to have seen the ghost town," Tracy told me. "I always wondered how a place becomes a ghost town."

"Played out mines. Worn out grazing land. Floods. Pestilence. You name it."

"How'd you like being the last person living in a town like that?"

"No, thanks. But if you were there with me it'd be OK. Let's go find Panhandle."

"What do you want him for? You going to ask him about Audra? I think we should talk to Sissy Dell. She's been here longer."

"Her too. Let's check on the cats."

We went to our cabin and rounded up our two wild cats and took them outside to play in the grass. They chased butterflies and each other and had a good time. Some rain clouds showed up and we put the cats back inside and headed for the dining hall.

"Do you think we should level with Panhandle and Sissy Dell?" Tracy asked. "Tell them what we've figured out?"

"Never give away more than you have to. What if one of them warns Audra off?"

"You got a point. Listen, you talk to Panhandle and I'll tackle Sissy Dell."

"Deal. But we'll have to find them first."

That proved to be easy. They were both behind the dining hall. Sissy Dell was hanging laundry on a clothesline near the croquet court: table clothes and kitchen towels and aprons. Panhandle was mowing the patch of wild grass that made up the croquet lawn. He was cursing to himself. I don't think he liked having to pull up the wickets to mow, and then put them back. Tracy went to help Sissy Dell while I followed Panhandle around and tried to keep him from cutting my toes off.

"How are the city slickers doing?" he asked me, while he took a breather.

"They're fine. We had breakfast with them."

"A second breakfast? What, we don't feed you enough here?"

"I don't want to risk losing my paunch. It makes me look distinguished."

"I wonder when the sheriff's going to let Lilly and the rest of the dudes go home."

"Who wants to go home?" I asked. "Tracy and me are having fun."

Panhandle shrugged. "You catch our little murderer yet?"

"I'll let you know when that happens."

"Good luck. If I was the killer, you're the last guy I'd talk to."

"I'll take that as a compliment. What do you know about your fellow buckaroos? Where they're from, what their folks do, whether or not they're triplets."

"They might all be triplets for all I know. I haven't been around them that long, you know? Hell, I got here the same time you did."

"Yeah, but you worked with some of these buckaroos before. A couple of years ago, right?"

"Sure. Sheepy and Breedlaw and Sissy Dell. The others are new to me."

"Any orphans in the bunch?"

"First you ask me about triplets, now you're asking me about orphans. Listen, I got a lawn to mow."

"You can rest a minute longer. I'm serious about wanting to know who might be an orphan." I offered him a cigar and he took it.

"Orphans? Are killers usually orphans?"

"Couldn't say. Who around here doesn't have parents, Panhandle?"

"I don't. Mine were killed in a bumper car accident at an amusement park. I swear."

"You're lying. I guess maybe I'll talk to Breedlaw. He should know something about the buckaroos."

"Sure, or talk to my uncle. Me, I don't know much. Hawk is a ladies man who's leaving. Drew is a wet-behind-the-ears bumpkin. Audra has a mean streak. Sheepy keeps girlie magazines under his bunk. Sissy Dell keeps a halo under her pillow. That's all I know."

"Audra has a mean streak? She seems as sweet as mountain meadow grass."

"That act's for the dudes. She likes playing the cowboys off against each other. She's a tease."

"Did you strike out with her? Is that why you think she's mean?"

"Naw. She ain't my type."

"No money? Too many curves?"

"What's with you, Mr. Detective? I'm just telling you what I know. You don't have to go getting personal."

"Sorry."

"Go jaw with somebody else."

Tracy had better luck with Sissy Dell than I'd had with Panhandle. She came over to me grinning like a bear full of barbeque. Apparently Sissy Dell wasn't all angel. She could be a gossip.

"It's got to be Audra," Tracy told me, making sure no one was near to overhear our conversation. "Her parents are dead. She talks about her mom like she was a saint. Her mom died when

Audra was a kid. Our buckaroo finished being raised in an orphanage in Nebraska. That's where the Rumdab's live."

"Perfect. What's the best way to handle this, I wonder? Do you think Audra would spill her guts to Breedlaw? Maybe not. I'm betting the old man, Primus Roan, could get her scared enough to talk. Let's give it a try."

Tracy wrinkled her freckled brow. "She'll go to prison, won't she?"

"Yeah, at the very least. She might get the gas chamber, though being a dame might help her."

"Maybe she's sorry she did it."

"Sure, and maybe Doc Rumdab is sorry he's dead. And his widow might be feeling some sorrow, too."

"You're right, but I still feel like an executioner."

"You do look good in black."

We went over to talk to Panhandle together. He'd finished mowing and was now scrubbing down his beloved grill with a Brillo pad.

"What is it now?" he asked us.

"We want to talk to your uncle. Can you set it up?"

"Talk to Breedlaw. He runs the dude ranch."

"Where can we find him?"

He took his attention off the grill for a moment.

"We talking about murder here?"

"That's right, but keep it under that silly hat of yours. Where can I find Breedlaw?"

"I don't know. He wanders around a lot. Listen, if you're ready to identify the killer, don't bother with Breedlaw. He hems and haws sometimes. Talk to Great Uncle Prime. He's the boy for action."

"Fine," I said, "give me his number and a phone."

"Coming right up, dude," said Panhandle. "Follow me."

He led us into the chuck house and to the kitchen. There was a wall phone. Panhandle dialed a number and handed me the receiver.

"Sadie will answer. Don't let her say no. She's awfully protective of Mr. Roan's time."

I put the phone to my ear and listened to it ring.

"Hello? Twin Roans Ranch. How can I help you?"

"Sadie? This is Axe Hatchett. You met us the other day. I need to talk to Prime. It's important."

"Mr. Prime's taking his nap. I can't disturb him."

"I understand, but I've been hired by him to find out who killed the dude, Dr. Rumdab. It's time to round up the murderer, and I need Prime to do his part. Never mind his beauty rest; you need to wake up your boss. Please. This is serious. If you won't wake him up I'll drive up to the house and start honking the horn."

"Don't you dare! If you really think it's that important, I'll get him up."

"Thanks."

I waited with the phone in my hand for what seemed an hour. It was probably five minutes.

"This is Prime Roan," an old voice finally said. I could tell he was trying to sound like everybody's boss, but he didn't have enough volume.

"Axe Hatchett. I know who killed Rumdab. Your employee, Audra. I want to bring her up to talk to you. We need her confession. What do you say?"

"Well, you're one of those hasty city boys, so give me a moment to think."

I waited half a minute. Then he started talking again.

"I need to call the sheriff."

"Do that, but let's not wait for him. I think Audra will talk if you and me get her cornered. That's my belief as a detective. I've solved a few murder cases."

"I trust you. I'll call Sheriff Fish. You go ahead and come on up to the house. Where is Audra?"

"Probably still showing the dudes the ghost town. As soon as folks get back, I'll grab Audra and bring her to you."

"Why would that poor girl kill the doctor?"

"It was personal. She thinks he killed her mom."

"All right. Round her up. I'll be waiting."

I hung up and turned to Panhandle, who, like Tracy, was eavesdropping.

"Panhandle, when are the dudes due back?"

"Pretty soon. I got to get lunch ready. They

should be back in less than an hour. I got trout to pan fry."

"Trout?" I asked. "I'm sorry I'm going to miss lunch."

"I'll save you a fish," said Panhandle.

"And one for me, too," said Tracy.

Tracy and I went out in front of the grub shack to wait for the dudes and the buckaroos. I burned a cigar and paced. Tracy sang a couple of cowboy songs.

"Are you sure Audra's guilty?" she finally asked me.

"I'd bet you a thousand dollars she's guilty."

"Keep your money, as if you had it. If Audra's not guilty — you know what? — you can buy me a string of pearls. I've always wanted pearls."

"OK. If I'm wrong and Audra isn't the killer, I'll buy you the best string of pearls oysters have to offer."

"Deal. But I hope nobody is a murderer. Are you sure Dr. Rumdab didn't commit suicide?"

"The sheriff doesn't think so. Rumdab was hit on the back of the head, remember. Look, I know what you're thinking. Tracking down killers isn't altogether fun. Pinning the crime on somebody you know is tough, even when they've tried to kill you — Audra might have fired those shots at us last night — but that's how it is."

"It's starting to rain."

"Let's walk up to the barn and greet the travelers."

I took Tracy's arm and we walked up to the corral in the rain.

"What if Audra won't confess?" Tracy asked me, as we ducked into the barn to avoid the water falling out of the sky.

"That's the spirit," I said. "Sink the ship before it's even taking on water."

17

When Tracy and me got to the barn, the big doors were open and we could hear Sheepy singing about darling Clementine. We walked in on him. The old cowboy was mixing up something in a big bucket and the barn smelled like a barbershop for horses.

"What kind of homebrew are you making?" I asked Sheepy.

He stopped singing. "Horse liniment. My own recipe. Witch hazel for a base, some wintergreen and juniper berry, and a splash of turpentine and a dash of pepper."

"What, no hooch? How about adding some gin? The horses would appreciate it."

Sheepy made a disgusted noise and spat into the straw at his feet. "They don't drink the stuff, mister."

"Say," Tracy asked him, "when are the dudes due back?"

"Well, they're up to the ghost town. Expected

back for lunch in about an hour, I figure."

"An hour?" I asked. "I don't want to wait that long. Could I talk you into saddling a couple of nags for me and the missus? We'll ride up and join the folks at the ghost town."

Sheepy narrowed his eyes at me. "Don't be calling my horses nags, even if that's what they are."

"I'll help you saddle them," said Tracy.

"Ma'am, I admire your riding, but nobody saddles my horses but me. I reckon you two dudes got a right to get your money's worth if you want to ride up to that ghost town. I got a couple of horses in the corral that are good and rested. I'll fetch 'em and saddle 'em up for you all."

He took a couple of bridles from pegs on the wall and headed out to the corral. In a few minutes, he came back leading a short-backed paint and a lean bay. He made short work of saddling them.

"I recommend the paint for you ma'am," he said to Tracy. "She's a might frisky."

"Suits me," said Tracy.

We led the cayuses out of the barn and mounted up. Sheepy followed us out and gave us directions to the ghost town.

"You take this road here for about two miles. Then you'll see an old wagon road—it ain't much—on your left. Follow it for another two mile and you'll be at the ghost town. Can't miss it. Bunch of broken-down old buildings. Watch them horses on that wagon road. It's mighty rocky, and

I don't want them horses getting stone bruised."

"Thanks for the help, Sheepy," I said, and Tracy and me started riding down the road.

We were scarcely out of sight of the barn when Tracy gave me a wink and kicked her paint into a trot. I did the same with my bay. It'd been a lot of years since I'd trotted a horse, and I bounced up and down like I was riding a pogo stick. Tracy stuck to her saddle like her pants were sewn to it.

"Come on, partner," Tracy shouted to me. She broke into a canter. "We've got a killer to round up."

"Don't sound so pleased about it."

I had my Browning High Power automatic stuck in my belt, and the horse's movements kept working it loose. I finally pulled it out and held it in my hand, just like some vigilante.

The day was heating up and burning off the rain clouds. We slowed our mounts to a walk again and in a short time came level with the old wagon road. It was nothing more than a couple of ruts choked with weeds and cluttered with stones. We turned up it.

"You can put your gun away now," Tracy told me. "We don't want to scare off Audra."

"Oh, yeah, you're right." I stuck the pistol back in my belt. "I'm trying to think how we're going to get Audra to cooperate with us. She'll likely know something's up. I'd hate to have her ride off into the hills, or—worse—get suspicious and decide to clam up."

"We'll think of something. Detectives are good at that kind of thing."

"Nice to know it's such a walk in the park."

It was slow going picking our way up the wagon ruts, but we finally came in sight of a gray log barn with half its roof gone. A little further on we came across some little cabins, a weathered church, and a false-fronted building that might once have been a saloon. It made me kind of thirsty for a beer and I told Tracy so.

"No drinking on the job," she said. "Audra might be a tough customer. I know she'll be wearing a gun."

"There's not going to be any gun play. We just need to accompany her back to the ranch without her knowing what's up."

We kept riding, passing a few more derelict buildings, and spotted some horses tied to an old hitch rail in front of the remains of another false-fronted log building. You could just make out the letters on a faded sign. It said "Assay Office."

"What exactly is an assay office?" asked Tracy.

"It's where they look at gold ore and other ores and determine what they're worth."

"I wish I'd brought my ore with me."

"Why, are we going boating?"

"I can row a boat...canoe?"

"I've heard that one before."

We got off our horses and tied them with the others. There were only four besides our own. Those would belong to Walter and Betsy, Hester, and either Drew or Audra. A pretty small party.

"What do we do now?" Tracy whispered to me.

"Why are you whispering? We're in the middle of a ghost town. What we do now is go look for our playmates. They're bound to be in one of these buildings. Just listen for the sound of cowboy songs."

We walked around the old place like a couple of tourists, though we didn't take any pictures. Finally, we heard voices coming from the old church. We moseyed over and stepped inside. It would have been dark except there was a big hole in the roof that let in sunlight. Betsy, Walter, Hester, and Audra were sitting on the remains of a church pew. We walked around where they could see us.

"Hey!" cried Betsy, "it's the rest of the gang. How'd you guys get up here?"

"We took the last stage," I said. "This is an interesting old town. You guys having a good time?"

"Sure," said Walter. He looked as happy as if he'd come to the church to attend a friend's funeral.

"Hi, Miles!" said Hester. "Hi, Trixie!"

Tracy stared holes in her.

"Hiya, Audra!" Tracy almost shouted. She had a big fake smile plastered on her face. "How are you doing?"

Audra started up like she'd been spurred.

"I'm—I'm fine," she said. She looked at Tracy

and then looked at me. I don't know what kind of expression I had on my face, but it must not have looked friendly. Audra turned pale under her suntan. "What are you two up too?"

"Nothing! Nothing at all," said Tracy. "We just rode up to join you guys."

"That's great," said Audra, recovering a bit. "We're getting ready to head back. We're having trout for lunch. Our pack mule ran off and Drew's out rounding it up. That mule runs off every chance it gets."

"What do you need a pack mule for?" I asked. "You didn't bring lunch."

"Our slickers and canteens are on that mule," Audra explained. "At least the rain's over."

"I could sure use one of those canteens," said Walter. "Walking around this dump has made me thirsty."

"I saw a saloon down the way," I said, helpfully.

"Wise guy," said Walter. "I don't suppose either of you brought any water with you."

"No," said Tracy, "we didn't think about it. We were kind of in a hurry. Detective business."

"I think I can handle this myself, Tracy." I said. "Why don't you go pick fleas off our horses?"

Tracy scowled at me. She's good at that.

Audra looked at the gun in my belt and at the no doubt disgruntled look on my sour mug.

"What's this about?" asked Audra.

"We know you murdered Dr. Rumdab," blurted Tracy. "We have all the evidence we need to get you arrested. Sheriff Fish is on his way. He might be at the ranch right now."

Audra stood up and it looked like she was going to make a run for it. I stepped close to her. Tracy came up beside me. Audra collapsed on the pew and put her hands to her face.

"What are you saying?" Betsy asked us. "Audra couldn't have killed anybody! She sings too much!"

"It looks like she's the killer," I said.

"I knew there was something wrong with her," said Walter. "Little Miss Sunshine."

Audra took her hands from her face. She was crying. "I didn't kill anyone! I didn't kill Dr. Rumdab, but it's partly my fault! I should have gone to Mr. Breedlaw. I should have talked to the sheriff."

"What would you have told them?" I asked.

"I—I can't talk."

"Sure you can. If you didn't kill Rumdab, who did?" I asked.

"I—Drew. Drew killed him. He found something out, something I shouldn't have told him. Drew's in love with me. Oh, I hate him!"

"Drew killed Dr. Rumdab?" Tracy asked. "But you were out in the woods with him that night. With the doctor. We found your hair."

"I was there, but I didn't kill anyone," said Audra. "Drew set the whole thing up. He said he was doing it for me!"

"I get it," I said. "You told Drew about your belief that Rumdab killed your mom."

"You know about that? How?"

"Never mind how," I said. "Tell us about what happened that night."

"Oh, God! I hate Drew, I hate him! Where is he anyway?"

"I'm right here," said a voice from the doorway. I hadn't even heard him riding back into town. "I caught the pack mule. Looks like I got back to town just in time to hear you blab your mouth, Audra."

I turned to face him; so did Tracy and Audra. Betsy and Walter and Hester stood up and turned to look at the boy in the doorway. He was wearing his revolver in a gun belt strapped to his waist. His hand was dangling dangerously close to the gun's handle.

"Throw that pistol of yours on the floor," Drew told me. His eyes looked crazy.

I shook my head. "No. My gun stays where it is. Give yourself up Drew. I don't know if you killed Rumdab or not, but you're going back to the ranch with us. We all need to talk to the sheriff."

Drew jerked out his gun and fired from the hip. My hat flew off. I pulled my pistol from my belt, thumbed off the safety, and fired off a wild shot. Drew fired again. I felt something tug at my shirt-sleeve. I aimed for his ribs, hoping to put him down but not kill him, and pulled the trigger. He dropped his gun and clutched his side. We were only fifteen feet apart. It took me four strides to reach him and I clouted him on the side of the head with my pistol. The kid decided to take a nap and fell to the floor. A cloud of dust rose up. I could hear the mule outside braying.

"Are you all right?" Tracy was at my side, fussing with my arm. There was some blood coming out of it, but not a lot. "Why do you always have to go and get shot?"

"I like donating blood. I'm very public spirited."

I turned to look at the others. They were all making noise, but none of them had been hit by Drew's bullets. That was a relief.

"Take off your belt," said Tracy. "I'll make a tourniquet."

"It's not that bad," I said, inspecting the damage. "The bullet just nicked a vein, tore a little flesh off. Help me tie it up with something."

Audra came forward and gave me her bandana and Tracy used it to bandage my arm.

"Let's take a look at Drew," I said.

Tracy and me knelt down by him. He was still knocked out. My bullet had hit him a little below the ribs on his right side. It was bleeding some, but the slug had gone straight through his baby fat without doing much harm.

"There's a first aid kit on the mule," said Audra. "Let me fetch it and we'll get you both patched up proper."

"Grab a canteen while you're out there," said Walter.

18

Twenty minutes later we were on the trail headed back to the grub house for a nice trout lunch. Audra had patched up Drew, though none too gently. He'd woken up and now complained of a headache. He had to keep one hand pressed to his bandage while we rode. I didn't much feel sorry for him.

Walter took the lead, armed with Drew's revolver and leading Drew's horse. Audra had taken off the bridle and rigged up a lead rope. We didn't want the kid killer to spur his cayuse and ride away from us. Drew came next, with me riding behind him, my pistol at the ready. The trail was wide enough that we didn't have to ride single file. Betsy rode next to her husband, occasionally bursting into tears. Tracy rode on one side of me and Audra rode on my other side. Hester took up the last spot and ate our dust. I hoped it wouldn't ruin her swell makeup. For once, she stayed quiet.

Tracy and me fired questions at Audra until we

got answers. We got the whole ugly story out of her.

"It was awful," Audra told us. "I don't know why I ever told Drew that I knew Dr. Rumdab was the quack who'd killed my dear mother. I knew that Drew had a crush on me and I guess I was hoping for his sympathy. It made me so angry to have that doctor at the Carefree Buckaroo. But I wouldn't have done anything to him. I barely even spoke to him."

"You didn't trick Rumdab into meeting you in the woods?" I asked.

"No, that was Drew's idea. He saw that the doctor spent a lot of time looking at Betsy, so Drew made me write a note — he wanted to make sure it looked like it was written by a girl. The note asked the doctor to meet Betsy out in the woods. He must have really had it bad for her, otherwise he wouldn't have dared going out in the woods at night, not with folks thinking that Brice had been murdered. Drew told me it was all just a joke, he was just going to scare the doc, for my sake. I don't know why I let him talk me into it. There was something scary about him, and I didn't dare say no. I should have gone to Mr. Breedlaw right then, I guess. Or maybe I liked the idea of giving the doctor a good scare."

"Did Drew somehow steal Betsy's earring?" asked Tracy.

"He found it. I didn't even know about it until later. Drew made me go out in the woods with him. He said he wanted me to be part of the joke…and he kept telling me he loved me. I tried getting him to leave me alone, but he wouldn't stop. I even asked Hawk to take him aside and give him a lecture, but Hawk was all show. He said he didn't want to interfere in my business."

"How did you get the note into Rumdab's hands?" I asked.

"Drew gave it to him, saying Betsy had asked him to pass it along."

"They never found that note," Tracy said.

"I guess Drew took it after he killed Dr. Rumdab," said Audra.

I'm sure Drew could hear us talking about him, but he didn't let on. He hadn't said more than two words since he'd come to in the church. He was being the stoic hero. I figured Fish was going to have some trouble getting Drew to confess.

"So," said Tracy, "you went out into the forest with Drew and waited for the doc to show up. What happened then?"

"It was awful," said Audra. "When the doctor saw us, he got mad and accused me and Drew of kidnapping him. Then, before I knew what was happening, Drew picked up a big rock and hit the doctor on the head with it."

"You didn't tell the doc about why you hated him?" I asked.

"I never had the chance once Drew picked up the rock. The doctor didn't have a prayer. That's when I ran off. I was afraid of Drew."

"For good reason," I said. "So, you ran off the trail and into the woods. We found some of your hair. We were able to match it when Tracy pulled that bubble gum trick on you."

"And now they'll think I'm the murderer," said Audra. "I just wanted to get away! When I was gone, Drew must have put a noose around the doctor's neck and strung him up. We all knew the stories about Jack the Roper, and we thought the Roper had killed Brice. I'm sure Drew thought he was being clever."

Drew turned in his saddle and shouted at Audra.

"Shut up!" he told her. "Just shut up. If it wasn't for your big mouth we would have gotten away with it."

"Shut up yourself," said Audra. "I didn't have anything to do with the killing."

"When you found out that Rumdab was dead," I asked, "why didn't you turn Drew over to the sheriff?"

"I was scared. Drew told me he had it all set up so that I'd get the blame for the killing. I had reasons for wanting Dr. Rumdab dead, and Drew had rubbed some of my perfume on a handkerchief and put it in the doctor's pocket. Besides, I thought that if Drew got arrested and then got let loose for some reason, he'd come and kill me. I know I shouldn't have helped him keep his secret, but I sure won't keep it now."

"I loved you, Audra," Drew wailed over his

shoulder. "Why can't you love me too? Look what I did for you."

Audra didn't say anything. I couldn't think of anything to say either. Murderers! You just can't get along with them.

We finally hove into sight of the ranch buildings. We stopped at the barn and Sheepy came out to attend to our horses. He smelled like that damned horse liniment. He raised his eyebrows when he saw my bandaged arm and the blood on Drew's shirt. He turned to Drew.

"What happened, son?" he asked the murderer.

"Nothing," said Drew, with lots of venom. "None of your business, old man."

"Why, you greenhorn whelp, what's you been doing to our dudes?"

Audra got off her cayuse and took Sheepy to one side. She whispered something to him and she looked like she was going to turn on the water works again.

Sheepy spat in the dirt. "If that don't beat all," he said, to no one in particular.

The rest of us got off our horses and led them into the corral. Sheepy gave me a look.

"Drew's a murderer, all right," I told him. "I gather that's what Audra was telling you about. She's OK. She just got mixed up with the wrong buckaroo. It's not her fault. Or, maybe it is. I've known dames that could twist a guy into pretzel shapes without even chipping their nail polish. Audra might have more to do with the murder than she's pretending. Who knows? I think the sheriff ought to grill her."

I went over to Drew. Walter was covering him with Drew's revolver.

"Put that thing away," I told Walter. "We're not going to have any trouble."

I hoped that was true. We all headed for the chuck house. Sheriff Fish's car was parked out front. His deputy, Lathe, was with him. So was Breedlaw, frowning like a sad clown.

Drew stopped about half way to the sheriff.

"I ain't going no further," he said.

I stuck my pistol in his back. "You want another bullet in you?" I asked.

Drew grudgingly walked the last few yards to the grub house.

Walter seemed to have cheered up some. He was talking to Betsy about some new invention he was thinking of. A saddle with a water reservoir built in. Tracy had lost her cockiness. Audra hung her head like she was headed for the gas chamber. I didn't think that would ever happen.

"What's all this about?" Fish asked me, walking forward to meet us and casually resting his hand on his service revolver.

"Drew here killed the doctor," I told Fish.

"That's a lie!" said Drew. "Audra killed him."

I took Fish by the arm and led him away a few feet so I could tell him what was going on.

"There's a story behind all this," I told him. "Dr. Rumdab was once Audra's mom's doctor.

She died and Audra has always blamed him for it. She told Drew the story and he killed the doctor to show how much he loved Audra. Dumb kid. I think Audra just got dragged into the murder. My guess is that she's innocent, but that's for you to figure out. I think you can get Drew to talk if you make him mad. Tell him what a chump he is."

"We'll get him to talk, don't worry," Fish told me. "Looks like you're a real detective after all. I appreciate what you've done for the county."

"Never mind that. I screwed up. I thought Audra was the killer."

"But you found the real one. Good job, dude."

"Thanks. If you don't mind, I'd like to take a whack at Drew when you question him. Some of these hard cases crack like eggs if you push them the right way."

Fish narrowed his eyes at me.

"City tricks?" he said. "Rubber hoses and all that? We don't do that up here."

"I'm not talking about anything like that. I just want to have a little chat with Drew."

"All right, but me and Lathe will be keeping an eye on you. We don't get much of a chance to interrogate killers in this neck of the woods. Could be you know a thing or two that can help us."

Breedlaw came over to us. So did Tracy.

"Are you really saying that Drew killed Dr. Rumdab?" Breedlaw asked Fish.

"Could be. We'll soon be finding out."

"I don't think there's any question," I said.

"Audra says he made her go along with the murder, but she may have turned the lad's head and put some ideas into it."

"It's terrible," said Tracy. "Drew tried to set Betsy up for the killing. But I think he also wanted to blame the murder on Jack the Roper."

"That fellow's dead," said Fish. "Jack the Roper's in the ground. I'm certain."

"Fine," I said. "This is some swell ranch you've got here."

"We try to make it a friendly place," whined Breedlaw. "Listen, I got a phone call to make."

He started toward the chuck house.

"I'm going to need to borrow your pantry again," Fish called after him. "No, come to think of it, we'll need a bigger space. We'll go out back to the picnic tables. I reckon you don't mind if we tell your buckaroos to stay away."

"Suit yourself," said Breedlaw, turning to face the sheriff. "I'll leave all this business to you." He apparently changed his mind about going into the grub house and headed for the barn instead. Maybe he was thinking of drinking some of Sheepy's horse liniment.

Walter and Betsy and Hester wandered off to their cabins, looking back over their shoulders every few yards to get their last look at an honest-to-God killer.

Fish, Lathe, me, and Tracy escorted Drew and Audra to the back of the chuck house. The sheriff turned to Tracy and took off his hat.

"Ma'am," said Fish, and there was an apology in his voice, "I reckon we got some man's work to do. Why don't you go on back to your cabin."

"No!" said Tracy. "I helped solve this case. I'm going to be part of the interrogation."

"Well, maybe you can take notes for us. Do you know shorthand? And would you mind making some strong coffee for all of us?"

"She's my partner," I told Fish. "She's not anybody's little secretary. What's wrong with letting her join us?"

Fish glared at me.

"No, sir. I'm still sheriff of this county and I'm doing things my way. Hatchett, you're just lucky I'm letting you be a part of things."

Tracy huffed like an angry bear. I hadn't seen that gimlet gleam in her red eyes since she'd been a waitress at Rocko's and some diner had complained about a fly in his coffee.

"Have it your way," she told Fish, "but come election time, I'm going to be running against you."

She turned, glared at me, and then stomped off toward our cabin.

Lathe had led Audra and Drew to a table on the back patio. He had his hand on his holstered gun. Panhandle was grilling trout. Sissy Dell was fussing with the picnic tables, setting out more food. They both gave the rest of us quizzical looks.

I went over to Panhandle.

"The killer of Rumdab is in custody," I told

him.

"Yeah? Who was it?"

"Your fellow buckaroo, Drew."

"No kidding? What happened to your arm?"

"Me and Drew had an old-fashioned gun sling-ing contest. They used to call me Billy the Kid."

"Naw. That's what they used to call me."

The trout was smelling good. I wandered over to the picnic tables. There were fried potatoes, a salad, some more damned Jell-O, and what looked like some kind of cobbler. I was getting hungry. I hoped we could wrap things up before lunchtime.

Fish chased away Panhandle and Sissy Dell

I sat down at the picnic table with the two cop-pers and the two suspects. It was nice and cozy. We could have started a card game. I made a sug-gestion to Fish.

"Don't you think you should talk to these two separately?" I asked. "They might have different stories to tell."

Fish pushed his hat up on his head and gave me a look that wasn't entirely friendly.

"Well, you may not believe it, but me and Lathe have a few other things to do. Time matters to us. I know you're a big city detective and all, but you ain't running this investigation."

"Do things your own way, by all means."

"Thank you. Did you ever spend any time in New York City?"

"I used to date the Statue of Liberty. It didn't work out."

Fish made a sour face and focused his attention on his deputy.

"Lathe," he said, "you're taking notes."

"Right, sheriff," said Lathe. He had his notebook and pencil ready to go.

I glanced at Audra and Drew. The girl looked scared to death. The boy was working hard to look tough.

Fish gave Audra an encouraging smile.

"Young lady, we'll start with you. Ladies first. Tell us what happened with you and Karl Rumdab."

Audra blew out her breath. She looked like she'd rather be anyplace else.

"Well," she began, in a tiny voice, "I knew Dr. Rumdab was coming to the Carefree Buckaroo. I saw his name on the reservations list. I could hardly believe it. He was the man who killed my mother."

"How's that?" Fish's eyebrows jumped halfway up his forehead. "How'd he kill your mom?"

"He was my mom's doctor. She got sick and Dr. Rumdab thought it was her kidneys. That's what he told the surgeon, but it was actually my mom's heart that was the problem. It killed her. I'd already lost my dad in the war. All of a sudden I was an orphan."

"I'm sorry to hear that," said Fish. "What'd you do when you found out Dr. Rumdab was coming to the dude ranch?"

"Nothing. Oh, I thought of things I might do to

him, but I'd have never done them. I'm not that way."

Drew let out a snort and opened his mouth to say something. Fish held up a hand to stop him.

"You'll get your turn to palaver, son," Fish told Drew. "Right now I'm talking to the young lady."

Drew clamped his mouth shut and glared at Audra.

"So you never planned on murdering the doctor?" Fish asked Audra.

"No. When he showed up, I just ignored him. Of course, he didn't recognize me. He hadn't seen me since I was a kid."

"Did you tell anybody on the ranch about what you knew of Dr. Rumdab?"

"Yes. I told Drew. I just needed to tell someone. Drew's been flirting with me and trying to make me his girlfriend. I kept telling him no, but he's persistent. He noticed I wasn't talking to the doctor and he wanted to know why. Somehow the story just came out."

"What happened when you told Drew your story?"

"He was real sympathetic. He said somebody ought to do something to the doctor. Then he came up with this plan to play a kind of joke on the doctor. He had me write a note pretending it was from Betsy. You know who Betsy is?"

"Yes. Go on."

"The note was kind of a love note, saying Betsy wanted to meet Dr. Rumdab out in the woods at night. I guess the note worked. The doctor showed up that night. I wish he hadn't."

"Were you two planning to kill the doc?"

"Oh, no! Drew said we were just going to scare him and make him look like a fool."

"So how is it you ended up killing him?"

"That was all Drew's idea. He hit the doctor with a rock. I couldn't believe it. I ran away, but I didn't dare tell anyone what'd happened. I was scared Drew would kill me too."

"That's not true, sheriff!" Drew shouted. "She's lying. She killed the old quack. It was Audra's idea to write the note and all. I just went along with it. I didn't know she was going to kill him."

"So it was Audra who struck the doc on the head with a rock?" asked Fish.

"Yes!"

"Why didn't you try to stop her?"

"It happened too fast."

"Why didn't you report the murder once it was done?"

"I don't know. I guess I was a fool. I guess it was because I was in love with Audra. I was trying to protect her."

"Let's see if I've got this right," I butted in. Fish gave me his sour look, but he let me go on. "Audra came to you and told you her sad little tale, then she pouted her pretty lips and jiggled her curves at you and you practically swooned. She wrapped you around her little pinky. You went along with the joke she had planned for Rumdab.

You went out into the woods with her."

"That's right. I didn't know she was going to kill him."

"Why'd she want you along?"

"I guess—I don't know. That's just how it was."

"Yeah? I think you're lying. Audra asked you to help her murder Rumdab, and you went along with it like a love-struck collie. You were supposed to bash in Rumdab's skull, but you lost your nerve. You ran away with your tail between your legs. You turned yellow. You didn't tell anybody about the killing because you were afraid this little girl would hurt you. Big strong cowboy!

"I've noticed how you're dressing more like Hawk. You want to be the manly cowpoke that dame's swoon over. But you don't have the nerve or the guts. You're just a little kid play acting. Nobody takes you seriously. I'm sure even Audra laughs at you behind your back. You're a pathetic little boy. You ought to be carrying a pop gun."

"Liar!" said Drew. "I got in a real gunfight with you, didn't I?"

"Sure, but you misjudged me. You thought I was some puffed-up city dude with a yellow streak as wide as your's. You thought I'd burst into tears and throw my gun on the ground."

"You think I was scared of that little doctor? You think I couldn't have killed him?"

"No. You would have wet your pants first. You couldn't kill a horsefly with a bazooka."

"He did kill the doctor," Audra broke in.

"Liar!" said Drew. "You did it. It was all your idea."

"You went out into the woods with Audra," I said. "You were supposed to kill Rumdab. You picked up the rock and then you lost your nerve. You couldn't do it. You probably started blubbering."

"That's not true, you lying little peeper!"

"Sure it is. You picked up that rock and your knees turned to water. No wonder Audra laughs at you behind your back."

"You're lying. You weren't there."

"No, I wasn't there, but I know what happened. You picked up that rock, and then you looked at that little runt of a doctor, and you couldn't make yourself kill him."

"You go to hell!"

"Sure. You picked up the rock, and then what?"

"I bashed in his head! I whacked him a good one! I killed the little bastard!"

"For Audra?"

"Yes, for Audra!"

"She knew you were going to kill him? It was her idea? You just went along with it like a moonstruck Cub Scout?"

"No! It was my plan. Audra wouldn't have gone along with it. She—"

He stopped talking. He knew he'd said enough. Too much. I turned to Lathe.

"You getting all this down?" I asked him.

"Every word," he said.

Fish took over.

"Drew, are you admitting to the murder of Karl Rumdab?"

"I'm not saying nothing more. I got my rights. I want a lawyer."

Fish turned to Lathe.

"Deputy, put the handcuffs on this boy. We're going to town." He turned to Audra. "You're coming too, miss."

The deputy cuffed Drew's hands behind his back. Fish and Lathe led Drew and Audra off to the sheriff's car. I watched them go. It was well-past lunchtime. I'd really worked up an appetite.

Almost as soon as the sheriff's car disappeared down the dusty road, folks started coming out of the woodwork. Sissy Dell and Panhandle did their best to save the delayed lunch. Walter and Betsy came out of their cabin and joined me on the patio. Tracy, still looking mad, came and sat down by me.

"How'd it go?" she asked.

"Duck soup. You were a big help with this case, cactus blossom. We'll work together again in the future. Just don't get shot up like I always do. Drew's a chump. He let me trick him into confessing. The boy makes a lousy killer. You hungry?"

"You bet." She was smiling now, her anger at Fish gone.

I went back behind our cabin, took off my shirt and washed the blood off my arm. My gunfight wound had stopped bleeding but I left the bandage on. Then I went into our cabin, said hello to the cats, and put on a clean shirt.

Panhandle and Sissy Dell served us our lunch. The trout was a little cold, but not burnt. We all ate our fill. The cobbler turned out to be peach, my favorite. I had a second helping. Breedlaw appeared out of nowhere and came over to me and Tracy.

"Mr. Roan wants to see you two," he told us. "The sheriff called him from town."

"Does Primus have a check for us?" asked Tracy.

"I imagine so," said Breedlaw. "I'll drive you folks up to the big house when you're ready."

"I know the way," I said. "We'll drive up there ourselves."

"Suit yourselves." Breedlaw went into the grub house.

Betsy came over to us, all excited.

"Did you catch the murderer?" she asked us.

"Sure," I said.

"All in a day's work, for detectives," said Tracy.

"I'm so glad! I feel safer now. Guess what? Walter's working on a new invention. It's a saddle with a big bladder under it. You can fill it with water, like a canteen, and it also cushions your ride."

"Sounds swell," I said.

Tracy and me walked over to our truck.

"Maybe Primus will give us a big bonus since we solved the crime so fast," Tracy said.

"Maybe. Or it could be he'll at least buy me a new hat. I've now got six bullet holes in it from three bullets. It's nicely ventilated for summer."

"You were wrong about Audra. Don't forget you told me you'd buy me a string of pearls if Audra turned out to be innocent."

"I haven't forgotten our bet. I'll go to the pawn shop as soon as we get home."

"Are you going to pawn something to buy my pearls, or are you going to buy the pearls at the pawn shop?"

"Both."

"Don't worry about it. You can owe me. Maybe you can give me the pearls for Christmas."

I parked the Studebaker in front of Roan's little palace and we went and knocked at the door. Sadie answered, smiling like a loon, and led us into the great room where Prime was pacing back and forth in his wheel chair.

"Mr. and Mrs. Hatchett," he greeted us. "I've taken the liberty of providing us with some libation. A fifty-year-old bottle of Happy Grampus scotch. Will you join me?"

"Sure," I said. "I guess you've heard the news."

"About Drew? Of course. I can't thank you and your charming wife enough for handling things so well. I've got a check ready for you. It's for a little more than what we'd agreed on, and you'll be getting your money back for the Carefree Buckaroo experience."

He wheeled his chair over to the sideboard and

poured out three drinks in big shot glasses. "You'll have to come get your drinks. I can't carry glasses and wheel my chair at the same time."

I went over and fetched me and Tracy's scotch. It smelled like Sheepy's horse liniment.

"I really can't thank you enough," Prime told us, while he sipped his scotch. "If there's anything I can ever do for you—" He left the sentence unfinished.

"Well," I said, "I have one favor to ask of you."

"Ask it."

"It's my hat. I've been wearing it for several years. But now it's got a bunch of bullet holes in it. Drew's responsible for a couple of them. I guess I'm lucky it wasn't my head. That'd be harder to replace."

"What's your hat size, young man?"

"Seven-and-a-half."

"What color would you like?"

"Gray, like this one."

"And the same style?"

"Yes. A fedora."

"Son, give me your address and I'll send you the best gray seven-and-a-half fedora money can buy."

"It doesn't need to be fancy. Just something to put on my head to keep the flies off."

"Whatever you want, son"

"I think brown would be better," said Tracy. "Axe has brown eyes."

"Brown it is," said Prime. He reached into his

cowboy vest and brought out a check. I stepped over to him and took it. It was for five-hundred-dollars.

"This is way too much," I said.

"No it isn't," said Prime. "You've saved me a lot of trouble. I'm thinking I should keep the dude ranch, maybe fix up the buildings, find some better horses, and hire some new buckaroos."

"Will you keep Panhandle?" I asked.

"My nephew? Yes, of course. I understand he's a good cook. He has a somewhat questionable past, but I'm a forgiving man. I'm thinking of keeping him on for the winter. We'll make a real cowboy out of him."

"It's been a real pleasure working for you," Tracy told the old man.

"Thank you for that. Now, if you don't mind, young lady, I have a favor of my own to ask."

"Ask it," said Tracy. "The answer's yes."

"Would you mind letting a broken-down old cowboy kiss your cheek? It would mean more to me than you can imagine."

Tracy colored up like a boiled lobster the way she does when she gets a compliment. She stepped forward and let Prime plant a wrinkled kiss on her cheek. Then she kissed him on each cheek.

"You've made my day, young lady," said Primus, with a goofy grin. I was almost jealous.

We thanked Primus and made our way back out to the truck. Tracy was as happy as a newborn filly.

"Think of all the money we have," she said, as we headed back to the Carefree Buckaroo. "There's Prime's five-hundred-dollar check, the money we're getting back from the Carefree Buckaroo, and the cash you still have from Miss Weatherby. We're rich. We can go on a second honeymoon."

"It's a little early to talk about anything like that," I complained.

"I don't think so. Maybe we can book passage on some swell ocean liner. If we're lucky, we'll get caught in a storm, the ship will sink, and we'll end up stranded on a desert island. Just the two of us, for weeks or months. Doesn't that sound romantic?

I shook my head. Sometimes that's all you can do with Tracy.

19

Our honeymoon was over. I drove us back to Quartz Quarry and almost fell asleep at the wheel. That's the mountains for you; the high altitude makes you tired but it doesn't catch up with you until you get back home.

The cats immediately fell asleep on the couch, a favorite toy between them. Tracy and me unpacked everything from the truck and carried the stuff up to our apartment.

"A nap would be nice," I said. "We've earned it, partner."

"A real nap."

"Listen, I've got a phone call to make."

Tracy dragged herself to the bedroom and I grabbed the phone in the living room. I figured Drew had been the guy who'd shot at us at the dude ranch, but I had another shooter to deal with now. I dialed Agnes Weatherby's number. She answered the phone herself.

"This is Axe Hatchett," I said.

"I'm so glad to hear from you, Mr. Hatchett. Are you back from your honeymoon? Did you have a good time?"

"Sure, it was swell. Very restful. Listen, is that goon Ned still living with you? I'd like to have a few words with him."

"Oh, dear. Dear me. Ned's not here. He's been incarcerated. Sometimes he drinks too much. Two days ago, a police officer pulled him over for speeding. I didn't even realize Ned—and Billy's old truck—were capable of any kind of speed. Ned was inebriated. He struck the officer, knocked him down. Then he took his pistol—the one he kept from the war—and shot out the tires of the police vehicle. He drove away, crashed into another car—a lawyer's—and tried to leave the scene on foot, after knocking down the lawyer with his fist. Ned's in trouble. Who knows how long he'll be in jail. I have refused to post bail for him. You see, Mr. Hatchett, I've finally learned how to say no."

"Congratulations."

I got off the phone as quickly as I could. Then I started laughing. I couldn't stop.

"What's going on out there?" Tracy called from the bedroom. "I'm trying to sleep. What's so funny?"

"The vagaries of justice," I said, and headed for the bedroom.

END

If you have enjoyed this book, please go to its Amazon book page and leave a short review. It will be most appreciated!

OTHER BOOKS BY THIS AUTHOR:

DEAD MAN LIMPING
[ISBN: 978-1-940469-00-3]

When 1950s private eye Axel Hatchett is hired by a delectable redhead to turn up her missing husband, Hatchett discovers that the man is not only still alive, but is armed, probably crazy, and is on a killing spree that may include Hatchett! But something stinks about this case—big time—and it's not Hatchett's pet skunk, Ambrosia.

GLIMMER IN A GLASS EYE
[ISBN: 978-1-940469-02-7]

After 1950s gumshoe Axel Hatchett is hired to protect a used car dealer from a threat of murder, Hatchett finds himself in a nest of rattlesnakes—literally! When the car dealer is bumped off, and Hatchett's prime suspect is murdered, the sleuth is forced to sift through a deck of also-ran suspects to solve the two killings before another corpse is added. And to make matters worse, he's falling for a mouthy waitress who works in a sleazy diner....

SLAYER IN A GRAY TOUPEE
[ISBN: 978-1-940469-01-0]

Rumpled 1950s sleuth, Axel Hatchett, is summoned to the Flinders Mansion to prevent a millionaire's threatened murder. After a fierce blizzard knocks out the power and closes the roads, Hatchett is trapped in the candle-lit mansion with an eccentric array of terrified guests and servants. The detective is determined to solve the case, but his only clue is a sinister gray toupee.

THREE CURSING BIRDS
[ISBN: 978-1-940469-03-4]

When thieves snatch a statue of the bird-headed Egyptian god, Thoth, and drop its owner from a third-story window, 1950s private detective Axel Hatchett is set on their trail. But wait! – there are actually three statues, and one of them may contain a treasure map! Hatchett enlists the aid of his hash-slinging fiancée and a snake-handling English professor to help solve the case of the three cursed birds.

KILLER BEAR FOR HIRE
[ISBN: 978-1-940469-04-1]

In all his years of sleuthing, snarky 1950s private eye Axel Hatchett has never faced a case like this: a bear trained to kill. Hatchett finds himself hunted by a deadly two-legged predator whose bullet comes unnervingly close to Hatchett's new wife, and that has Hatchett seeing red! Armed with a revolver and his caustic wits, Hatchett is out to solve a grizzly killing, or die trying.

JACK THE ROPER
[ISBN: 978-1-940469-05-8]

1950s private sleuth, Axel Hatchett, is looking forward to a relaxing, belated, honeymoon in the high lonesome at a dude ranch. But before it can start, Axe tries to solve the disappearance of a purloined bunny, ending up with a cracked skull, and it's not the rabbit's! When he and Tracy finally arrive at the dude ranch, Axe expects nothing worse than bad beans and bucking broncos. Instead, bullets and a hangman's noose await the newlyweds.

FLICKERING TORCH SINGER
[ISBN: 978-1-940469-06-5]

When 1950s detective, Axel Hatchett, steps up to help his friends with their failing night club, he has no idea that he's embarking on a twisted, flickering road that will lead him to put his life on the line to protect a smoldering torch singer from a murderous stalker. And that's before he tangles with the infamous gangster, Pennsylvania Dutch!

BOOK CLUB DISCUSSION QUESTIONS
(For People With Discerning Minds and Exquisite Taste)

1. How did you experience this book? As a dude, or as a buckaroo?

2. Describe the main characters — did you meet similar outlaws at the last dude ranch you stayed at?

3. What was particularly engaging about the plot, and why?

4. What passages struck you as funny, and why?

5. Who is your favorite character? Your second favorite character?

6. Was the ending satisfying? If so, why? If not, why not?

7. After reading this novel, are you now yearning for a vacation in the Wild West?

ABOUT THE AUTHOR

Steven LeRoy Nelson is an award-winning humorist whose short fiction has appeared in *Alfred Hitchcock Mystery Magazine*, *Ellery Queen Mystery Magazine*, *The Leviathan*, and numerous other publications.

Visit him at his website at:

www.stevenleroynelson.com